JACOB

THE BURNETT BRIDES
BOOK NINE

SYLVIA MCDANIEL

The Cowboy lost his memory and the wanderer longs to forget her obligation.

Jacob Burnett knows the danger of the rodeo. He's witnessed many a cowboy flying through the air, but this is his dream. He's going to win or die trying. And dying is a possibility when he's thrown from a bull and hits his head.

Hannah is living her best life as a runaway. With no job, her home is a ragged old camper visiting every nature reserve before she must return to New York City and fulfill her commitment. Everything has been great until the night she rescues a cowboy who can't remember his name.

Intent on keeping her identity a secret, she fights the growing attraction between her and the handsome bull rider with amnesia. Then he remembers everything.

Can the matchmaking ghost help Jacob realize the beautiful wanderer rode into his life for a purpose?

Are you signed up to receive my new book alerts? Don't be left out! Sign up at my website www.Sylvia.McDaniel.com

CHAPTER 1

*A*t the Texarkana rodeo, Jacob Burnett sat inside the steel box, otherwise known as the chute, ready for the longest, most dangerous eight seconds, on the back of the bull. Beneath his legs, he felt the quiver of the bull's muscles. The animal would soon give him the ride of his life.

Eight seconds. That was all he needed. Eight seconds of bucking bull, and at the end, the Winner's Circle. Eight seconds to prove to himself and the world that he could be a rodeo star and that he wasn't crazy for having dreams of something besides the Burnett ranch, which he loved. But this was him. This was his dream.

A rope was wrapped around his gloved palm tying him to the back of this beast. Taking a deep breath, he signaled he was ready and the gate swung open. The beast exploded into the arena.

Raising his left arm in the air, he spurred the animal hoping for a better score, and the bull raised his back legs in protest. Spinning, bucking, snorting in anger, the animal tried to fling him off its back. After flying up in the air, he slammed down on the bull's back and knew he'd be walking funny for a few days.

The jarring blow sent pain radiating up his spine. The screams from the crowd became a muted sound as he hung on for dear life, his focus on staying on the back of this wild animal.

The bull shook and flung him up again, but this time he landed sideways on the animal and he could feel himself falling.

No, not yet. The buzzer hadn't sounded. It was too early. Too soon.

Knowing he'd be crushed by the fifteen-hundred-pound animal if he didn't let go, he released the rope. He fell to the earth with a slam, his back and head bouncing off the dirt.

The screaming of the crowd faded as his brain shouted get up and run, but his body refused to move. He lay there in the dirt, his mind repeating the command.

Run before the bull does even more damage. Before the animal kills him, gores him to get its revenge.

He couldn't get in any air and the lights started to dim, the crowd noise withered and he feared he was going to pass out right here on the floor of the arena.

The earth shook with the pounding of the bull's hooves, and at any moment, he expected to feel the bull's horns piercing his flesh.

Where were the clowns? Where were the cowboys to guide the bull out of the arena?

And then the beast was gone.

Paramedics rushed to his side. "Jacob, can you hear me?"

With a gasp, his lungs filled with air and the dimness of his vision disappeared. The crowd had gone silent as they waited for some signal from him. Had he been unconscious?

"Yes, I got the wind knocked out of me. I couldn't move." He gasped like he'd smoked a pack of cigarettes every day for twenty years.

"Can you move your fingers?" the paramedic asked.

He wiggled his fingers. Thank God, he wasn't paralyzed.

"Is your head hurting?"

"My whole body hurts," he groaned.

Right now his body seemed to light up every place he'd hit the ground, letting him know he would hurt for several days.

"Follow the light," the paramedic said, holding up a pocket-size flashlight.

The bright light hurt and he cringed as he tried to follow the glare with his eyes. All he wanted was to curl into a ball and wish the pain away.

"I think we should take you to the emergency room to be checked out," the paramedic said. "I think you have a concussion."

Oh hell, no. They would contact his next of kin and the entire Burnett family would be up in arms that he'd gone rodeoing without telling anyone. Aunt Rose would have him cleaning pigpens for months for taking such a chance. The old woman protected them more than his mother had ever done.

"No, I'm going to be fine," he said, feeling nauseous. He had to get out of the arena so the next rider could take a chance on his seconds of glory. "Sit me up and let me get my bearings."

"Are you sure?"

"Yes," he said. "How long did I last?"

The man shook his head and sighed. "Just under five seconds."

Five seconds of agonizing hell that wouldn't even get him on the scoreboard.

With a curse, they helped him sit up. "All this for less than eight seconds."

The crowd roared when they sat him up, believing he was going to be fine when, right now, he wasn't even certain he could walk.

The paramedic helped him to his feet and the world spun around him. They both watched him closely and if he showed any weakness, they'd be hauling his ass to the back of their ambulance. There would be lights and sirens and people asking him all kinds of questions.

Not the ride he wanted tonight.

All he needed was some backwater hospital to call his family and let them know what he'd done. His butt would be on the line if they learned he'd come here alone and gotten hurt.

Oh no.

"Can you walk off on your own?"

Sure he could, just like a drunken sailor walking the plank.

"Yes," he said, determined not to show any feebleness. He'd sit in his truck and bemoan the fact that he'd lasted less than five seconds.

As he bent down to pick up his hat that lay in the dirt, he almost passed out. Taking a deep breath, he walked toward the gate of the arena, the paramedics by his side. His vision was blurry and even the sound of the crowd was mottled.

The people in the stands cheered for him and he waved his hat uncertain that he would be back. But then again, this was his dream, and so far it was hard work. Two broken ribs, a cracked wrist, and now a second concussion were all that he had to show for his attempts to go professional. A couple of belt buckles, but that elusive dream of the big time seemed just out of his reach.

Some bull seemed to always cut his time short or didn't put on the show the judges wanted. This sport was a young man's game and he was getting too old to continue.

At the gate leading to the outside world, the paramedics studied him.

"You're sure you're fine?"

"Boys, I'm going to drink some water in my truck and then I'm going to head home. Oh, and I may take an Advil to help ease my bruised bones."

With a sigh, the older paramedic handed him some paperwork.

"You have to sign this release saying you realize you may be concussed and should be taken to the hospital, but you declined."

He grinned, thinking of how many of these releases he'd signed.

"Hand me a pen," he said.

The paramedic handed him a pen and he scribbled across the paperwork. His handwriting wasn't even recognizable.

"Safe travels home. Don't hesitate to go to the hospital if you need to," the paramedic said.

"Sure," Jacob replied, hoping it didn't sound as condescending to the man as it did to him. There was no way he was going to a hospital. The memories of being there with his family had him cringing at the very thought.

Walking away, the worst pain was between his legs where

he'd slammed down on the bull's back. He'd have the ice pack between his thighs tonight. Tomorrow he'd walk like he had a stick up his butt and wonder why in the hell he did this.

Climbing into his truck, he found the bottled water he kept in a cooler and quickly took two ibuprofen. He had a four-hour drive home along winding roads with deer and skunks and other small creatures. He should get going, but he just wanted to rest for a bit.

With a sigh, he leaned his head back against the seat and closed his eyes. He just wanted to relax for a few minutes before he started home. He just needed a little time before he got on the road.

Four hours later, he awoke to an empty parking lot. The moon was high in the sky, and for a moment, he considered just staying here and spending the night in his truck. He could lock the doors, lie down, and sleep until morning.

But tomorrow was Sunday and his newest niece was being baptized in the church. He didn't want to miss Joshua's youngest daughter's baptism. His brother now had two little girls and he adored them more than he'd ever believed possible.

Cursing, he gazed around him. It would be early morning before he reached home. But he needed to go.

He felt the back of his head and gasped at how tender the knot was. If he'd hit any harder, he might have cracked his skull.

Time to go home and reevaluate his life. Maybe his dream wasn't for him after all. Maybe it was time to consider retiring from bull riding.

After starting his truck, he pulled out of the parking lot and turned onto the highway toward the ranch. Wanting something to keep him awake, he listened to music while watching the road for critters.

Two hours later, he noticed his gas tank was getting low as he came through the small town of Giselle, Texas. It had one red light and two gas stations. Both were closed, but he could still pump gas since he had a credit card. He pulled into the one pump on his side of the road, grabbed his credit card out of his wallet, and went to fill up. The little town had rolled up the sidewalks and no one was around.

As he finished pumping gas, a truck filled with young men pulled into the station behind him. Another truck pulled in front of him, blocking him in.

This couldn't be good.

Reaching into his truck, he tried to pull out the pistol he carried, but they jumped him before he had a chance to unlock the gun case.

They pulled him out of the truck.

"What you got here?" one man asked, grinning.

They were druggies. He could see the wild look in their eyes and knew they were going to rob him. They were in need of their next fix and he was their latest target.

"My wallets in the truck," he told them. "Take it and go." It held a thousand dollars in cash, which could get them all higher than a windmill. He'd be on the phone canceling the credit cards before they were out of the parking lot.

They laughed as they started ransacking his truck. They found the gun case and the man hit him with it.

"You were going to use this on us?"

"No, I was going to warn you away with it," he replied, wondering where the local sheriff was at this time of night.

"This truck's pretty nice," one of the men said. He started it up. "We could sell the parts."

They found his wallet, his phone, everything.

The leader looked through his wallet and found his driver's license. "I'd like to know who I'm about to kill."

Fear spiraled through Jacob as he stared into the man's eyes. They held a soulless coldness that told him this man would kill him in an instant and not lose a night of sleep over it.

The leader looked at him, grinned, and then he punched him. First, in the face and then kicked him when he fell to the ground.

They were going to kill him. Remembering what he'd learned as a child, he closed his eyes and pretended that he'd passed out.

A car sped by, horn blaring.

"Let's get out of here," one of the men yelled.

The bull hadn't done the job, but they were going to finish what the animal started.

He felt a blow to his head and the lights went out.

CHAPTER 2

*H*annah Newhouse sang along to the CD player in the old SUV she'd purchased, enjoying her freedom. The road was dark and narrow and there were very few cars coming or going. Trees lined the sides and shadows played along the highway.

Peace filled her and she knew that she should be afraid, but she wasn't. It was late, but as long as the old car kept running, she'd be fine.

Sometimes you had to do drastic things to make a statement, and buying this old jalopy of a car along with the turquoise camper she pulled behind it would shock her family. Good. They needed to be tossed into the chaos she was creating.

Maybe it would wake them up to the damage her father had done to their lives.

Some dreams couldn't be ignored and visiting the sites where Georgia O'Keefe painted had been her goal since she started painting. No one was going to deny her this dream any longer. As a painter, she wanted to walk the same ground her idol had walked, visit her museum in Santa Fe, and even set up her own easel to see if she could capture the beauty Georgia created.

Halfway there, she prayed the old car would make the journey and she loved the little trailer she pulled behind the car. A big bright rainbow was painted across the back.

No hotels, no phone, nothing but cash in her pocket; she was untraceable. And she loved the peace that gave her.

One month was all she needed before she would fulfill her obligation.

Sure her mother would be worried, and her father would be furious, but she didn't care. If she had to do the impossible task he'd asked of her, then she deserved this trip. He'd not only told her no, but *hell no* when he learned of her plans.

She'd even dyed her blond hair in case he had detectives searching for her. Now she was a take-charge redhead. Nothing and no one was going to stop her.

Look out New Mexico, here she came, and along the way, she'd charted out several places in Texas that she wanted to paint. So far, she'd visited Kentucky and Tennessee, and now she was crossing from Louisiana into Texas.

It was long past midnight and she estimated she would reach Pedernales State Park by early morning. After she got the camper set up, she would rest and then spend two days painting. After that, she would go to the Davis Mountains then the Guadalupe Mountains before she went to New Mexico and traveled north to see her idol's home in Abiquiu.

On the way back to New York, she planned on seeing Palo Duro Canyon if she didn't go on to the Grand Canyon. She had two months before she had to be home to do her father's bidding. If somewhere along the way, she didn't grow a spine and tell him no.

But how could she? Her family would be devastated. Her sisters and her mother would suffer because of her selfishness, as her father put it. Damn him. For a smart man, he pulled some stupid stunts.

The headlights shone brightly on the road ahead as she sang along to Pink. The trees looked like ghosts standing along the edge of the road.

An image appeared on the highway.

Suddenly, she slammed on the brakes and the trailer behind her swerved. Oh no. A man stood in the middle of the asphalt, blood on his face, waving his arms.

Crap! She didn't have a cell phone, not even a burner phone. Nothing. What if this was a trap? The only weapon she had was a Taser beneath the seat.

Easing off the brake, she slowed her car, the trailer no longer swaying, as her heart pounded at the sight of a cowboy in bloodied clothes, trying to protect his eyes from the glare of the headlights. She reached beneath the seat, grabbed the stun gun, and prayed she could remember how to use the thing.

Sure, she'd read the instructions, but that had been over a thousand miles ago.

Pulling up beside him, she cranked the window down, her hand on the weapon. She didn't say a word. She wanted him to tell her what was wrong.

"Howdy, ma'am," he said. "I can't seem to remember where I'm at. Can you tell me where I am?"

Oh no, he must be a druggie. "It's three a.m. and you're not far from Longview, Texas," she said. "What happened to you?"

"I don't rightly know, ma'am," he said. "I woke up in the grass on the side of the road and just started walking. I think I've been walking for hours," he said.

Starring at him, he looked beat up. He had a black eye that was almost swollen shut and his gait was funny. "It looks like you were in a fight."

Confusion crossed his face and he groaned. "I don't know."

He needed a doctor. But she didn't know him, and all the television programs she'd watched where someone picked up a hitchhiker and disappeared slammed into her memory.

Could he be another Ted Bundy?

"What's your name?"

He gazed at her, his eyes blinking as he shook his head. "Can't remember."

"Have you been doing drugs or drinking too much?"

"No, ma'am," he said with confidence. "But I hurt all over."

"Check your pockets," she said.

His hands moved over his pockets and he turned them out. Nothing. Maybe he'd been robbed. Maybe even now the robbers were waiting in the bushes to attack again. She glanced into the darkness, fear spiraling through her.

What should she do?

It would be inhumane to leave him out here on the road. He needed help. He could die. But she was taking a huge risk. Could she die?

With a sigh, she put the Taser beneath her leg, hoping it didn't turn on and shock her into tomorrow or even an early grave.

As much as she feared him, she couldn't leave a man with blood trickling down his face on the side of the road.

While glancing around the darkness, fear scurried down

her spine. Time to decide and get on down the road in case someone else was hiding in the bushes.

"Get in," she said. "I'll take you to the next town."

She watched as he walked in front of her car and then opened the door. She had to move the trash from where she'd been snacking so he could sit. Quickly she rolled the window up and as soon as he shut the door, she hit the locks. If someone else was out there, they were not getting in.

"My name is Hannah," she said, remembering the advice her self-defense instructor had said. Always let your abductor know that you're a person with a family and a life. "I'm on my way to New Mexico."

"Oh," he said. "Nice to meet you, Hannah."

She put the car in drive and they moved toward the next town. She'd watch his every move while trying to keep her eyes on the road. The Taser lay between the door and her thigh.

"Where do you live?"

Shaking his head, he groaned. "I don't know. I don't remember much of anything."

The man had either been out drinking or he was seriously injured. But he didn't smell of alcohol or even like he'd been out partying somewhere.

"Do you have a car?"

"I'm not sure," he said. "It's the weirdest feeling. I think I was going home, but that's all I remember."

Glancing over, she noticed he wore a very expensive pair of boots and had on a nice pair of jeans that hugged his body. If he'd been cleaned up, he would be a handsome cowboy. The hat on his head had to be worth several hundred dollars, so if he was doing drugs, he must be selling them.

He wasn't a poor down-on-his-luck kind of cowboy.

Great, just what she needed was to have the police stop her and find him in her car. What if he was wanted? She drove the speed limit knowing she couldn't afford to be pulled over. That would be a one-way ticket back to New York and two months of hell.

"There's a wet wipe in the glove box if you want to use it on your face. You've got blood and dirt on your cheek. I think I should take you to the emergency room."

There was no way, she was going in. She would just drop him off and pull out of the parking lot before anyone could see her and be on her way again.

"No hospital," he said.

Most druggies liked going to the emergency room where they could load up on pain pills. Where an ER doc would grant them their every wish to get them to leave and pray they never returned.

"What if your memory doesn't come back," she said. "Don't you think it's odd that you don't know who you are? A doctor needs to take a look at you."

With a sigh, he leaned his head back against the headrest. "Do you have any ibuprofen?"

How did he know to take a painkiller if he couldn't remember his name or what he'd been doing when someone obviously kicked the shit out of him.

"Yes, in the same glove box where the wet wipes are," she said. "And there's a cooler with bottled water in the back."

He turned to the back seat and she heard him hiss with pain. "I think one of my ribs is broken. Maybe more."

How would he know that?

"All right," she said. "Another reason to go to the ER. Are

you certain you weren't in some barroom fight? Or some kind of domestic violence?"

"No, to the ER, and I don't know what happened to me. It feels strange when you wake up in a ditch and don't remember a thing," he said with a sigh. "I'm going to take a couple of ibuprofen, and if it's all right with you, could I just lean back and rest for a bit? I'm so tired. I just want to close my eyes and stop feeling so bad."

"Sure," she said. "When we reach the next town, I'll wake you up."

"All right," he said. He took the pills, swiped his face with a wipe, and then pulled his hat down over his face.

Soon she heard him breathing in a normal rhythm and she sighed with relief. He was asleep.

When she reached the next town, she tried to wake him, but he turned away from her. Just great. She had a strange man in her car who would not get up. He was beaten and bloody and she feared what would happen when she stopped. What if he died in her car?

One more town…

Finally, the sun was beginning to rise and she was only thirty miles from her destination.

As the eastern sky turned pink, she gave him a shake.

"Huh?" he asked, glancing around with wide eyes.

"I've passed about five towns and you've slept through them all," she said. "Time to go."

Shaking his head, he ran his hand down his face. He looked around at the tiny town.

"Where are you going?"

"I'm headed to Pedernales State Park," she said, wondering why she was telling him this.

"That's a beautiful place. I've been there. The fishing is really good," he said.

It was weird the things he remembered and how all his pertinent information was gone like his name and address. Or was he faking it?

Was this a ploy to let her guard down and then he would attack?

She pulled up to a diner and put the car in park. She turned to face him wanting him out of her car now. Time for her to continue on her dream journey.

"If you can remember Pedernales State Park, why can't you remember your name?"

With a shrug, he gazed at her. "I don't know. My head is pounding and I'd just like to lie down and not be moving."

This was not her problem.

"I'd really appreciate your help, ma'am. I know this must be scary for you, but it's damn frightening for me. I'm out in the boonies and I don't know my name or where I'm at."

"You should go to a hospital," she said.

"No," he replied. "Hospitals give me the creeps. Don't know how I know that, but they do. Something bad happened there and I don't want to go back."

That was weird.

"Are you running from the law?"

"I have no idea," he replied honestly. "Look, I promise that I won't hurt you. You've been kind to pick me up. If you want me to get out of your car, I will, but you're kind of my lifeline right now. If you help me, I'll make it up to you somehow."

She reached over and yanked his shirt sleeve up.

"What are you doing?"

"Looking for needle tracks. I don't want anything to do with anyone who has a drug problem."

A smile crossed his face. "I don't do drugs. I can promise you that."

"And you know Pedernales State Park?"

"Yes, ma'am," he said. "I know I've fished there."

How could he know that and not know his name? It just didn't make sense. And this man was not going to ruin her trip. This was her last chance for her dream to happen.

"Why are you going there?"

"I'm a painter and I want to paint the landscape. The falls, the area. Why?"

"Maybe I could show you some good spots to paint," he said, shaking his head. "How I know this and I can't remember my name I don't understand. Who are my people?"

If only she could get on the internet and research amnesia. But she had no links to the outside world. Nothing. All the cords to her father had been cut and, hopefully, he wouldn't find her.

She pulled out the stun gun from beneath her hip and pointed it at him. "Do you know what this is?"

He gulped. "A Taser."

"Don't think I won't hesitate to use this on you. Try anything and you'll find this thing jabbing your broken ribs, and then I'll leave you behind in the dust. Do you understand me?"

"Yes, ma'am," he said, smiling. "I don't want any trouble."

"Well, somewhere along the road, trouble found you," she said, putting the weapon underneath the seat. "And stop calling me ma'am. I'm twenty-four not sixty."

A smile crossed his face. "All right, Hannah. I was just trying to be respectful."

"Be respectful by staying on your side of the car and not giving me any problems," she said.

"Yes, m—Hannah," he replied.

"Now, what am I going to call you? I can't just say *hey you?*"

With a sigh, he shook his head. "I'd like to call myself something too."

"How about Cowboy," she said. "You're dressed like one."

"I think I am one," he said, gazing at her as she pulled the car out onto the road again. "I think I went to a rodeo. But what happened after that, I can't recall one bit."

CHAPTER 3

*J*acob could see that Hannah was exhausted when they reached the state park. After she'd paid the gate attendant, she located their camping spot and backed the little trailer onto the concrete slab.

"You're good at this," he said.

"I've done it a few times," she said. "Look, I'm going to lie down and rest. The camper will be locked. You can stay in the car or go hiking or do whatever you want, but you're not coming inside with me."

He was fine with that. He just wanted to sleep. Nausea held him in its grip and his head pounded like he'd experienced a five-day drunk. Reaching up, he ran his fingers along the back of his skull and found not one knot but two.

Someone had knocked the crap out of him.

"Does the back seats go down?"

"Maybe," she said as she got out of the SUV.

Knowing he should be helping her, but not wanting to move, he sank down at a picnic table and watched her set up the trailer.

The sun was climbing in the sky, and a hot wind blew out of the north. All he wanted was to close his eyes and die for several hours.

"What day is it and what time of the year?" he asked wondering if that would give him any clues as to why he was out walking on that lonesome dark stretch of highway.

"It's September," she said.

"I did go to the rodeo," he said, his forehead drawing into a frown. "I know I did."

She turned and gazed at him, her brows raised in a questioning gaze. When he didn't say anything else, she finished leveling the trailer.

"There's a blanket in the back of the car," she said. "You can curl up in the back seat or the cargo space. I don't care which. I'm going to sleep now," she said.

He watched as she disappeared inside the camper and he wanted to go with her. It was such a strange feeling to be dependent on someone you didn't know, that you'd only just met. But right now, he couldn't call anyone if he tried. Right now, she was his everything.

"Hannah," he called. "Do you have a phone?"

"No phone," she said.

That was odd. You'd think someone traveling alone would have a cell phone in case of an emergency. You'd think he would have a cell phone—wait, he did. Or at least he had.

She closed the door to the trailer and he heard the lock slide into place. The woman had nothing to fear from him because he felt weaker than a newborn kitten.

Once again he was by himself and he didn't know who he was or anything about himself. It was a strange, uncanny feeling. One he didn't like.

Already he could feel his body demanding that he rest and he hadn't done anything.

Opening the back end of the SUV, he found it stuffed with painting supplies. An easel, paints, canvas, everything she would need. Somehow he knew if he moved this stuff, she was going to be upset with him.

There were several paintings that looked like they had been laid down to dry. Though he didn't know much about art, he could tell she was really good. Better than any painter he'd ever seen. The landscapes were filled with vivid colors and you wanted to step into the painting and be in the flowers and stream she'd drawn.

He didn't dare touch any of this stuff. He found the blanket and slid to the backseat where he gingerly removed the cooler and all but dropped it on the floorboard.

Then he lay out in the backseat with the windows open to cool the warm car.

His head was still hurting and fear held him in its grip. What if his memory didn't return? What if he was seriously injured and would soon die?

Closing his eyes, he pushed through his memories, trying to grasp anything that would tell him what he did for a living, anything about his life. Nothing. Just like a blank canvas, nothing but white, ready for the splash of life that would tell him about himself.

A sudden painful flash filled his brain and he groaned as he remembered the pain. A gas pump. Men surrounded him, a fist flew toward him, and then it was gone.

Something bad had happened to him. He curled up on the backseat and soon drifted off to sleep.

When he awoke, he was hungry, and of course, he couldn't remember the last time he'd eaten.

Glancing out the windows, he realized it was almost evening. Sitting up, he felt better, but still not great. Going outside, he walked around and gathered firewood. Soon he had a little blaze going in the fire ring. Then he looked through the cooler.

Not much, but there was a package of hot dogs. If only he had a wire to cook the meat on. There was a sooty grate, but it looked like it'd never been cleaned. Getting out her wet wipes, he cleaned the metal the best he could and then laid a couple of hot dogs on it to cook.

The camper door opened and a sleepy-looking Hannah stepped out.

"You found the hot dogs," she said.

"Yes, I hope you don't mind, but I thought I would cook us up a couple for dinner," he said.

"No," she said. "In fact, I have some chips and other things we can have with them."

She went back into the little travel trailer and brought out buns and plates and even hot dog relish and mustard.

Soon, they were both sitting at the picnic table eating as the sun sank beneath the horizon. Food had never tasted so good. It wasn't until this moment that he realized how hungry he was.

If someone was searching for him, this would be the second night he was gone.

"I remembered something," he told her.

She stared at him, her emerald eyes gazing at him intently.

"There was a gas station. Some men surrounded me and I remembered feeling pain."

With a sigh, she shook her head. "Sounds like you were robbed."

"Maybe," he said. "But why and how did I get there? Who am I?"

"No name?"

"Nothing," he said, never feeling so lost before. What if he remained this way the rest of his life? How could he find people who were searching for him if he didn't remember his name?

She rose from the table. "Did you get enough to eat?"

"Yes, thank you," he said. "If we had marshmallows, we could roast them on the fire."

A grin spread across her face. "We do. I brought them because I wanted to taste roasted marshmallows and I wanted to make s'mores. I have all the fixings."

She ran back into the trailer and came back out with her hands full.

"You've never had s'mores?"

"No," she said. "Do you remember how to make them?"

He couldn't stop his smile. "I haven't forgotten s'mores. Do you have a coat hanger or something we can cook the marshmallows on the fire with?"

"Yes," she said and hurried back in.

When she came back, she had a long wire coat hanger. He put several marshmallows on it and then put them over the fire. Soon they were blazing with the inside gooey and the outside crisp.

"Give me a graham cracker," he said.

She handed him one, and he put the crispy marshmallows on the cracker. "Now for some chocolate."

He put the dark square on the marshmallow and then put

23

another marshmallow on top of it, then the second graham cracker, and handed it to her. The chocolate melted between the scorching-hot marshmallows.

She took it from him and opened her mouth. "Oh," she said. "This is so good."

As he made himself one, the memory of his mother and father and his brothers all sitting around a campfire eating s'mores came to him. It was a happy memory and suddenly it gave him hope.

"I have a family," he said. "Brothers, a mother, and a father. They must be crazy with worry."

A grin spread across his face. He was starting to remember bits and pieces of his life. Maybe soon, he could call someone who knew him. Maybe soon, he would tell Hannah good-bye.

"Are you married?" she asked.

Searching his brain, nothing came to mind. "Not sure."

"If you are, your wife must be crazy with worry," she said softly.

"I wish I knew," he replied. "I would never do this intentionally to someone."

Hannah didn't say anything and he didn't know what her silence meant.

The sound of something moving in the brush had them turning and gazing to see an armadillo creeping into their campground.

"Look," she said and ran inside. When she came back, she had a sketchbook in her hand and a pencil.

"Don't touch it," he said. "They carry bacteria that can make you sick."

How did he know this?

Sitting on top of the table, she gazed at the animal and began to sketch the creature.

"You're starting to remember more," she said.

"Let's hope so," he said, feeling like he was adrift in a vast sea. So much was missing and he was ready for it all to come flooding back.

The armadillo sniffed around their campfire, and not finding any food, wandered back into the brush.

Gazing at her in the firelight, he couldn't help but think she was beautiful. It was really the first time he'd looked at her. Last night, his head had been hurting so badly that he could hardly see. Last night remained a blur of pain and misery. Last night, he'd been afraid of being left on the highway.

Why in the world had a woman like Hannah taken a risk by picking him up? Her long auburn hair curled around her full breasts. And in the darkness, he could see her emerald eyes gazing at the animal. Full pink lips, high cheekbones, and a long nose were framed in her heart-shaped face. Rounded hips and long legs that a man would love to have wrapped around him completed the picture.

"What about you? Why are you traveling alone?"

It was unusual to see a woman out driving that late at night by herself. Especially pulling a camper on her way to New Mexico.

"I'm an artist and my favorite painter is Georgia O'Keefe. I'm on my way to visit her museum, her home, and even paint where she painted. It's been my dream for a long time and I'm not giving it up for anyone."

There was such determination in her voice. How neat to

SYLVIA MCDANIEL

have a dream like that and be going for what you wanted. Did he have a dream?

Nothing came to mind.

"What does your family think of you traveling alone?"

She licked her lips. "They're fine with it."

Something about her statement didn't feel right. A woman going somewhere without friends or family seemed unreal. Especially in these dangerous times.

"Where are you from?"

"Florida," she said, not looking at him but continuing to draw the armadillo.

Why did he think she was lying? The tone in her voice was not what he'd expected to hear from someone from Florida. The woman was hiding something, but he couldn't really press her. He was there because of the generosity of her heart. Otherwise, he didn't know where he'd be.

With a sigh, he realized his ribs were beginning to ache once again and there was still that dull throb in his head. The food seemed to have helped him feel better, but he was still not doing great.

An owl hooted in the night and he knew he would not last much longer. Already his body was longing for the back seat.

"If you don't mind, I'm going to walk down to the men's bathroom and take a shower. Then I'm coming back and going back to sleep."

She glanced up at him.

"What are you going to do if you don't remember who you are before I leave Texas?"

That was something to consider. His family was obviously here, but where?

"Maybe we can go by the sheriff's office and see if anyone has filed a missing person's report on me?"

Her eyes grew wide and she tensed. "Sure," she said.

He got the feeling that she didn't want to visit the sheriff. It seemed that Hannah was hiding something, but that was her business and not his. He had enough problems at the moment.

As he stood, a spell of dizziness overcame him and he swayed, fearful he was going to pass out.

"Are you all right?"

"I'm fine," he said, knowing he had to be.

"Goodnight, Hannah," he said, turning to walk down the road to the showers.

"Goodnight," she called.

When he got down to the showers, he pulled off his clothes and was shocked. Oh yes, he'd most definitely been in some kind of fight. And yes, he had a broken rib. In the morning, he'd see if Hannah would bind up his sides for him.

Stepping under the warm spray, he sighed. Who in the hell was he and when would his memory return?

CHAPTER 4

The next morning, Hannah cooked eggs and bacon over the fire outside the camper. She thought the smell of frying bacon would wake Cowboy, but it wasn't until the eggs were ready that he finally stepped out of the backseat of the car.

"Good morning," she said.

"Good morning," he replied.

"Do you feel better?"

"A little," he said.

She noticed that he wasn't wearing a shirt and realized he must have washed it. It was hanging on a nearby tree and he walked over and grabbed it off the mesquite branch.

"Do you have something we can use to bind my ribs? I think two of them are broken," he said.

The man's nude chest was rippled with muscles in all the right places and she could see bruising where someone had obviously beaten him. The urge to run her fingers over his chest and ribs almost overcame her.

What was wrong with her?

"Let me look," she said, escaping into the trailer where she found some supplies.

A few minutes later, she came back with a pillowcase and scissors. She cut the pillowcase into one long strip and then she stepped in close to him.

The smell of soap and water and a manly scent teased her and she breathed deeply.

In her hands, she had a large safety pin to hold the wrap in place.

"Sorry, this is the only thing I could find," she said.

Laying the pillow case against his smooth skin, a tingle of heat spiraled through her at the feel of his rugged muscles beneath her fingers. Her breath became quick and she shook her head. This had never happened before when she'd touched a man, and yet, she had also never felt a man's chest before.

Hannah was as virginal as they came. She'd never really had much interest in boys, not even in college. All she wanted to do was paint. In college, she'd dated, but just never found anyone that she wanted.

Now, her father had other plans for her.

"Tighter," he said as he gasped with pain, his face contorting.

"Are you sure," she said, not wanting to hurt him.

"Yes," he said between gritted teeth. "Don't ask me how I know this, but I know it has to be tight."

Standing this close to him, it was all she could do not to run her fingers across his broad shoulders and feel the strength she imagined beneath her touch.

Finally, he said, "Enough."

She pinned the cloth together, hoping it would stay tight.

His face was white as he slipped his shirt over his wrapped ribs.

"Maybe you should take some aspirin. Sit down and I'll get them for you," she said. "Also breakfast is ready."

Walking into the trailer, she glanced around at her little home, searching for the cabinet where she kept medicine. It was in the bathroom and she quickly grabbed the bottle and brought it out. She set it in front of him then dished him up some eggs.

"Sorry, I don't know how to make toast on the grill," she said.

"No problem, maybe tomorrow morning, I can show you," he replied.

Pouring him a cup of coffee, she sank down on the picnic table across from him.

"Maybe you should stay here at camp today and rest. I'm going to take my easel and paints and find the waterfall," she said.

She'd seen pictures online and knew she wanted to paint the area. The rock formations from the river were interesting and beautiful and she couldn't wait to see if she could come close to making the painting as gorgeous as Mother Nature had sculpted the area.

"It's only about a mile," he said. "If you want to go to the main falls area where the cavern is located, it's a longer hike."

It was weird that he remembered places he'd visited.

"Day after tomorrow, I'm heading up to the Guadalupe Mountains," she said. "Have you ever been there?"

His crystal blue eyes narrowed and she could see him trying to remember.

"I don't know. It sounds familiar, but then again, I can't

remember where I came from. I can't remember my home address."

If this had happened to her, she would have been glad not to remember where she came from, but then again, it had to be weird. Today, she felt more relaxed around him. She wasn't afraid that he was going to harm her and she wasn't certain that was a good thing or not.

Cowboy had been an extreme gentleman that was polite and hadn't tried to put any kind of moves on her. That was hard to come by these days. She wondered how far he would travel with her. Right now, she was enjoying his company.

"I've got about another week in Texas before I head up into New Mexico," she said.

"I'll have to make a decision before then if I want to continue with you."

"What kind of decision?"

He didn't want to go to a hospital. Would he want to speak to the sheriff? Hopefully, by then his memory would return.

"Whether or not I should go to law enforcement and see if anyone is searching for me."

"Your wife must be crazy with worry," she said.

Sitting there, his face scrunched up as he tried to remember. "I don't think I'm married. I could be wrong, but it doesn't feel familiar. You would think I would know. I don't have a wedding ring, but that could have been taken from me."

Hannah finished her eggs, slammed down her coffee, and glanced at him.

"Are you certain you're up to a hike?"

"Yes," he said. "I want to watch you paint the falls. I wish I had my fishing pole with me. I'd catch us some crappie, which would be delicious over a fire."

Stunned, she stared at him. "I like fish. Don't know how to catch them, but the man I bought the trailer from left a pole and a tackle box. You're welcome to use them."

Maybe it would be good for him to get his mind off his problems and do something besides sit and wonder who he was.

A smile spread across his face. "I'd love to. Maybe fishing will help me relax and my memory will return."

Hannah had no doubt that it was going to take time and rest. But it would be fun to have someone by her side today. She'd been gone for almost two weeks, and while she'd enjoyed her adventure and her travels, it had gotten lonely.

No phone calls, no communication, and yet she wouldn't go back. Not yet. The best was yet to come.

Picking up a bleeding man in the middle of the night was not how she had planned on meeting anyone on her adventure.

"Let's get ready and go. I've got a full day of painting ahead of me," she said, excited to get started. Feeling the paintbrush in her hands as she put splashes of color on the canvas made her calm and filled her with a sense of purpose.

Going inside the trailer, she found the fishing pole, the tackle box, and even the hat she liked to wear when she sat outside in the sun.

Carrying everything out, she handed him the fishing gear and then went to the back of the SUV where she put her backpack on that contained her paints, brushes, and everything she needed. Then she grabbed her easel and a stool she liked to sit on.

"Let's go," she said and locked the car and the trailer.

She really wasn't certain that he was up to this, but they

walked down the road to the river and the waterfalls. Once they reached the water, they followed a trail that led up the mountain toward the falls.

"It's not far," he said.

"You've been here before, so you can't live too far away," she replied. "I would think your home would be close."

"I wish I knew," he said. "I like to fish and hunt and…" he paused, his face changed like he was expecting a message. Then he sighed. "It's gone. I thought I was getting a memory of where I lived."

She turned to him. "For today, don't push yourself. Give your brain some time to heal. Just relax and enjoy."

When she first picked him up on the road, she'd had doubts that he was being honest with her, but now she knew he was telling her the truth. The man was so frustrated that his mind had gone blank and she couldn't even begin to imagine the feeling of not knowing who she was and where she lived.

The hike was rocky with cedar trees and bushes along the way.

"Watch for snakes," he warned.

She wanted to see a rattlesnake. And if she could, draw the viper, but she didn't know if that would be possible. She doubted the snake would agree to sit for her.

At the top of a rise, they reached the rocky falls. Not really a waterfall, just white water rushing over the rocks with a rock enclave cut out inside the hill. It was a beautiful spot and she quickly set up her easel and put the blank canvas up for her to work on.

Before she began, she sketched out what she wanted to

show in her painting, fearing as always that she wouldn't get the colors brilliant enough.

For a few minutes, Cowboy watched her.

"I'm in awe," he said. "Hell, I can't draw my horse."

Stunned, he glanced at her and smiled. "I have a horse."

That was fitting.

"I'm going to relax and drop a hook in the water," he said. "I'll be right down here if you need me."

"Great," she mumbled. She'd already taken out her sketchpad and was busy working on how she wanted to portray the area.

An hour later, she glanced at the two sketches she'd drawn, torn between which one to paint. Finally, she decided on the one without the man. All she needed was for her father to think she'd made this trip with a man. She'd be in so much trouble. Even more than she already was.

Suddenly she heard Cowboy yell and she rushed toward him, afraid he'd fallen into the river.

"Look," he said. "We're going to eat good tonight." He held his pole up and she saw a fish squirming and flipping on the line.

At least he was having a good time, and hopefully, relaxing.

Back at her easel, she sank down on her stool, and like always, became wrapped up in the scenery as she sketched it first on the canvas and then began to add the paint. She was so involved in what she was doing that she didn't hear the park ranger walk up behind her.

"Ma'am, that's beautiful," he said.

She whirled around to face him, wishing he had not disturbed her concentration.

"Just wanted to let you know we're expecting severe storms here this afternoon. Be sure to keep an eye on the sky," he said. "If we sound the siren, everyone has to come down to the bathrooms. That's the tornado shelter."

"Thank you," she said. "I wouldn't have known."

The man walked away, but she saw him stop and talk to Cowboy and he nodded.

Once again, she went back to painting and pushed all thoughts of storms, Cowboy, and even her family, from her mind as she concentrated on turning the canvas into the beautiful scenery.

At the first rumble of thunder, she glanced up to see Cowboy standing in front of her.

"We better go; it's going to storm," he said.

Just then the wind tossed her canvas and he grabbed it before it could blow away. The paint was still wet and she would have to do repairs, but at least it wasn't in the river.

Quickly, she took down the easel, put her paints away, and slipped the backpack over her shoulders.

"Let's go," she said, gazing at the sky, worried they wouldn't get back to the camper in time.

They hurried as the wind began to blow hard and lightning streaked across the sky. Thunder rumbled and shook the ground.

The first raindrops began to fall when they reached the car.

She threw the canvas in the back, and just as she pulled off her backpack, the pour hit.

Shutting the back of the car, she ran toward the trailer.

The doors to the car were still locked. Cowboy was trying to get in. Lightning struck a tree nearby and she screamed.

"Get in the trailer," she said. "Hurry."

He ran to the trailer and she moved to let him inside. Water dripped from his hat, his shirt, and even his pants were soaked.

From the bathroom, she pulled out a towel and handed it to him.

"Here," she said. "Dry off."

The trailer was small with just a bed, kitchenette, table, and a small potty. No shower. And this hunky Cowboy was taking up so much space.

She glanced at the bed and thought about her Taser out in the car. But she really didn't fear him.

"Have a seat," she said. "I'll make us something to drink."

"Coffee would be great," he said. "I'm a little chilled."

It couldn't be good for him to be cold. Not with him having amnesia. "Why don't you go in the bathroom and take off your shirt and pants? You can wear my bathrobe."

"Are you certain?" he asked. "I don't want that stun gun used on my broken ribs." A grin spread across his face, showing he was teasing her.

"Stay away from the bed and you'll be just fine," she said.

A few minutes later, he emerged from the bathroom and she could tell he was really nervous.

A giggle escaped her. "Cowboy, you look mighty cute in my bathrobe with your boots on. Don't you think you should take them off?"

"No," he said. "You're a lady and I'm not going to subject you to my stinky feet. They could smell good, but I'm not taking any chances with these old boots."

Those were old? She knew they were expensive because she'd researched western boots one time for a class project.

JACOB

The man dressed nice.

"How are we going to cook our fish," she asked.

Glancing out the window, he looked at the sky. "This storm won't last long. It'll probably blow over in thirty minutes. The worst is already over."

She thought of the way lightning had hit the tree not far from the camper. That she hadn't been prepared for.

"Where did you get the camper?" he asked. "It has New York tags. I thought you were from Florida."

Oh, dear. Even the SUV had New York tags.

"I go back and forth between New York and Florida," she said. It wasn't a complete lie. Her family had a beach home in Florida they spent a lot of time at.

He sat at the table and she could see he was nervous. It was like he felt cramped. And he did take up a lot of space in her little home.

"I need to get the fire started and the wood is wet," he said. "There are fish to clean and then we can fry them up with some potatoes and onions."

He glanced up at her. "Do you have potatoes and onions?"

"A few," she said, thinking of how she'd stocked the camper when she reached New Jersey. That was a few miles ago.

His fists clenched and unclenched.

"Are you nervous?" she said with a grin.

"Yes," he said, chuckling. "I'm sitting here in my underwear, wearing a woman's bathrobe. It's a little uncomfortable."

She laughed. "Relax. I'm not going to jump your bones and you're not going to jump mine unless you want electricity soaring through your body."

A grin spread across his face and he gazed at her. Suddenly

37

his eyes widened. "I was riding a bull yesterday. I was in the rodeo and I fell off and hit my head."

That was good, but he hadn't gotten two broken ribs and bruises from falling from a bull, had he?

"It's coming back," he said. "You were right to tell me not to think too hard today. Maybe tomorrow even more will come back. Maybe I'll soon know who I am. Then I can call someone to come and get me."

Warmth filled her, and she wanted to hug him, she felt so excited, but she didn't.

"That's great," she said. "I'm so glad your memory is returning."

CHAPTER 5

This morning while Hannah loaded the camper and put things away, he made them breakfast. When he offered her a plate, she turned her face away.

"I can't," she said. "I just can't eat right now."

In the early morning light, her color was off. She looked white and he wondered what was wrong with her. She'd been fine last night.

"Are you feeling okay?"

She swallowed hard but didn't respond. "We've got to load up and get on the road."

After he finished off the eggs, he tried to help her, but she knew where everything went and all he could do was hand her the chairs and other camping gear.

"Are you ready?" she asked.

"Yes, but what's wrong?"

Shaking her head, she walked away. Suddenly she leaned over and threw up.

"That's not good," he said, bringing her a paper towel and a bottle of water.

SYLVIA MCDANIEL

"We've got to go," she said. "I need to stay on schedule."

There was a schedule? First he'd heard of that, but then she was bound and determined to get to some small town in New Mexico he'd never heard of.

A warm breeze blew as she hooked up the SUV to the trailer.

"Let me," he said and lifted the trailer onto the hitch and locked it down.

Her face was white.

"What's wrong with you?"

She glared at him like he was the stupidest man on the planet and he suddenly knew. "Oh."

"Yes, oh," she said. "The curse arrived, and with it, a migraine, stomach ache, and cramps that would kill an ordinary man. And a mood that will make anyone near me wish that they were dead."

A grin spread across his face. "Sorry, I don't have sisters, so I don't know about those things."

"Hey, another clue. I have two sisters," she said. "You're lucky."

Cowboy wished he had sisters because then he thought he would understand women better. They could help him with the opposite sex.

From her expression of misery, he felt bad for her.

"Look, you took care of me. Let me take care of you," he said. "I can drive us to the Guadalupe Mountains."

She gazed at him. "You don't have a driver's license."

"Not on me," he said. "But I have one, I'm sure. I know how to drive."

For a moment, she bit her lip, undecided. But something told him, he'd driven a vehicle with a trailer before.

"I'll drive the speed limit. I'll be extra careful and you can lie down in the back and sleep," he said.

With a sigh, she gazed at him. "This is all I have. Do me a favor and don't wreck it. I'm going to take a migraine pill and sleep. You can drive."

She trusted him and that filled him with a happy glow. It had been two days since she'd picked him up, and every day, he felt stronger and better, and it was just a matter of time before he was back to normal.

Even the knots on his head were going down.

"Scout's honor, I'll do my best to get us there safely," he said.

"Figures, you were a Boy Scout."

"I think so," he said. "Now you lie down. I'm just going to check everything so we don't get pulled over. We'll be pulling out of here in five minutes."

Shaking her head, she went into the trailer and came back a few minutes later with a pillow and a blanket.

Walking up to him, he could see she really didn't feel good.

"I've taken a migraine pill, so no driving for me. It's all up to you," she said.

He grinned and got behind the wheel while she climbed into the back.

For a moment, he stared at the old dashboard. Why did this look so wrong?

"Hey, where's the navigation system?"

"In the side pocket of the door. It's called an atlas," she said. "A highway atlas. Do you know how to use it?"

The woman had nothing electronic that could hook her up to a satellite or anything that would help someone searching for her.

He laughed. "Yes, my father used one. He made us boys learn how."

Frustration filled him. How in the hell could he remember incidents like this, but not know his name? It was so damn excruciatingly painful not to know who he was and yet every day he remembered something more about his past.

With a sigh, he started the SUV and pulled out the atlas. She had drawn a red line to where they were going. Five hours was what he calculated on Interstate 10.

"Are you ready?"

"Yes," she said, sounding groggy. Those pills must take effect quickly.

"And we're off," he said, putting the car in drive. The trailer gave a little jerk as he pulled it out of the parking spot. He'd enjoyed spending the last two days here, catching fish and resting. And his body was beginning to heal, but just not fast enough to make him happy.

Mainly he wanted his brain back to normal to give him the information it had stolen from him. Having ribs that didn't hurt would've been nice too.

As he pulled out onto the highway, he glanced back and saw she had drifted off to sleep.

Over the next few hours, the terrain changed and became more of a desert and not the Hill Country of Texas. After five hours, he pulled the car over before they went into the campsite area.

Not knowing his name or having a wallet or anything to ID himself, he felt so disoriented. She better be the one to sign the paperwork for their camping spot.

Groggily, she woke and stretched.

"Are you feeling better?" he asked.

"Yes," she said. "Are we here?"

"Yes, and I don't know what to tell them. I thought you should drive us in," he said.

She nodded, sat up, and then stepped out of the car.

"Wow," she said. "Look at the mountains."

"All I could think was that I missed the trees."

A smile graced her face. "There is beauty in all types of landscape. Georgia O'Keefe showed me that."

Whenever his memory came back and he was settled, he was going to look for this painter he didn't know. He wanted to compare Hannah's paintings to hers and see where she got her inspiration.

Hannah could paint. There was no doubt about that.

After she got behind the wheel, she paid their entrance fee in cash and then they drove to their assigned spot.

As soon as she backed the trailer in, he jumped out and started setting it up. Since she still didn't feel good, he wanted to help in any way he could.

Right at sunset, he found wood and started a fire in the ring.

"You're good with the fire," she said, plopping into a comfortable chair she'd set up around the campfire. "I wonder what you do for a living."

"Good question," he said, wishing all the pieces would fall into place like a giant jigsaw puzzle.

"I'm starving," she said. "We probably should have stopped at a grocery store before we reached here. We're beginning to get low on supplies."

He hated that he was eating all her food and was not contributing gas, food, or even helping to pay for the campsite each night.

"Do you have any ground beef? I could rustle up a cowboy goulash."

"What's that?"

"It's onions, tomatoes, beans, and ground beef," he said. "Or I could make us tacos."

"Let's make the goulash," she said. "I like your cooking."

At least he was earning his way a bit. And while she looked like she felt better, she still didn't appear to be one hundred percent. Plus, he was certain she wouldn't feel like cooking tonight.

"You know if I had money, I'd help pay for things," he said. "Hell, if I had a debit card or a credit card, you wouldn't have to worry."

What happened to his wallet? His credit cards?

"I know," she said, frowning. "When I reach Santa Fe, I'm going to sell some of my paintings in the square."

"Were you planning on doing that before I came along?"

"Yes and no," she said. "It's been my desire to sell some of my paintings or have an art show. I just didn't know when and where."

He nodded.

"I tell you what," she said. "Black and white nudes sell very well. Why don't you pose for me? Not full frontal, but just your back. Women love a naked man's back and butt, especially when he's wearing a cowboy hat."

A grin spread across his face. "You want me to pose nude for you?"

"Yes," she said. "You have the physique. It would be great. We'd make some extra money to help pay for groceries."

Shaking his head, he felt a blush spread across his cheeks. "I do owe you a lot."

"That would pay off your debt," she said, grinning.

"Let me think about it," he said, feeling uneasy being nude around her. The woman was gorgeous and what if…Oh no, that would be so embarrassing. And selling his body for art had never been something he'd considered before. He didn't think, anyway.

The sun was sinking and he wanted to make her a meal. It was one way he could help with his clothes on.

"First, let's have supper," he said.

She went into the camper and a few minutes later came back with the meal ingredients.

"I have some flour tortillas we could have with it," she said.

"Do you have any cheese?"

"Let me look," she said and disappeared back inside.

When she returned, she was carrying bowls and she had the cheese.

"We've got enough food for about two more days and then we'll need to find a grocery store," she said.

Sinking down in a nearby chair, she watched as he fried up the onions and ground beef.

"You're a good cook over a fire," she said.

"Thank you," he replied as he mixed in the canned beans. "My dad was a good cook. I don't remember my mother's cooking."

With a sigh, he wished he could remember who his father was. But he knew the man liked to fish and he cooked well and that he had two brothers. Were they searching for him?

He hated that his family would be worrying about him, but he couldn't remember their names, phone numbers, or even where they lived.

The sun sank below the horizon, bathing the area in a

golden array of colors. It was gorgeous and Hannah grabbed a camera and took several photos.

Art was her life and he knew she lived and breathed painting, and he'd only known her for three days.

"Later, I'll download those and I can use them if I decide to paint one of the sunsets," she said.

But she had no computers that he'd seen. Nothing in her trailer. Would she wait until she got home, wherever that might be? Or had she hidden her computer where it couldn't be seen?

"Were your parents artists?" he asked, wondering about her.

"Oh no," she said. "My father is in finance and my mother is in social climbing. They're both excellent at what they do."

A grin spread across his face. "My mother was as well, though it didn't get her far. Pretty much destroyed my parents' marriage." How Jacob knew his mother was a social climber, he didn't know, but he was certain it was what ended his parents' happiness.

Hannah shook her head. "My mother has it perfected down to an art. Know the right people, throw glamorous parties, and always make certain the press is there. Give to the right charities, and be the head of women's groups in your area."

"Did you have to go to a lot of these parties?"

She laughed. "Oh no, children were to be seen and not heard. Until you were old enough to be a debutante."

In the darkness, he watched as she rolled her eyes.

"Sadly, I was a rebel who only wanted to paint. I started very young and took lessons and then in high school, I won a national contest. After that, I knew what I wanted in life, and I've been working toward it ever since."

The fire popped and he couldn't help but wonder if her family approved of this trip. She'd said yes, but from the sounds of her life with them, they would not want her roaming alone.

"And they approve of you traveling the countryside, painting?" he asked again.

She laughed. "Oh no. Anything to do with me being an artist makes me a bohemian gypsy. My father has done everything he could to make me grow up and get a real job. Work in finance, real estate, banking, or even marketing, but not painting. That's the worst."

The goulash was done and he spooned out some for her in a bowl. "Where did you go to college?"

He handed her the bowl then spooned up his own dish. The smell called up memories of three little boys sitting around the fire, waiting on their father to feed them. Were they his brothers and what were they doing?

With a shake of his head, he turned his attention back to Hannah.

"School of the Art Institute of Chicago," she said. "Graduated with a fine arts degree. My professor told me I was the best student he's ever had and encouraged me to do what I loved. And against my family's wishes, that's what I'm doing, painting."

That was an expensive school, probably the best in the country. Even he recognized the name.

The thought of doing something you loved and going against the family's wishes seemed familiar. Was there something he'd done that his family would not approve of?

"This is delicious," she said. "Not the boring stuff, our c—"

She almost admitted to having a family cook. Why did he get the feeling that her family lived in a mansion with servants? So how had she ended up living in a camper? He'd bet odds they didn't know she was on this trip.

"Do you still live with your parents?"

"Not any longer," she said.

Not any longer because she was living in this camper. Could the high society girl be living in a run-down beat-up camper without her parents' approval?

Why did it feel like his mother and Hannah probably had a lot in common? Worried at the thought, he grew nervous. He feared what he would remember about his family when his memory returned.

Could Hannah have come from a wealthy family like his mother?

Finishing the goulash, she gazed up at the stars. "Wow, look at the heavens. So many stars you can't see when you live in the city."

Gazing up, he stared in amazement. There were millions of little lights shining down on them.

Just then a howl echoed off in the distance.

"What is that?" she asked, turning toward him, her emerald eyes wide.

"A coyote," he said, knowing instinctively.

Gazing up at the stars, he thought of how his family had existed for generations gazing up at the stars on the B… ranch.

With a sigh, he leaned his head back and closed his eyes. The name had been so close and then gone.

"What's wrong?"

"It almost came to me. My family has lived for years on the B...ranch," he said. "It was right there and then it disappeared."

"Good, you're starting to remember things. Soon you'll know and then we'll part ways," she said. "Maybe even before I head off to New Mexico."

"Yeah," he said, not certain how he felt about that. She would be traveling alone again and he would return to his life. But right now, she was his only connection to the outside world and he needed her.

Gazing at her, he couldn't help but wonder what the touch of her skin felt like. Would it be soft and silky? How would her lips taste? Would he enjoy kissing her, and how would she respond to his kiss?

And yet, what if she came from a family like his mother's? What would he do then?

With a groan, he stood. "I'm going down to the showers to clean up," he said. "Will you be okay here alone?"

"Yes, I'll do the dishes since you cooked," she said.

"Sounds good."

"Hey, thanks for driving us here today and letting me rest," she said.

"I'm just glad you're feeling better," he admitted. He'd been worried about her.

"Me too," she said. "Tomorrow morning, I paint."

He nodded. "Goodnight, Hannah. Sleep well."

"You too," she said as she watched him walk toward the showers.

Did the woman have any clue how she made him feel? How at this very moment, he had to leave to take a cold shower. Also, he needed to wash out his clothes and hang them up to dry.

His ribs ached, but he continued to push himself to get better.

But right now, he didn't want to leave her. Right now, he needed her.

CHAPTER 6

*T*ravis knew what he had to do. It was Wednesday and Jacob had not been seen since early Saturday morning when he pulled out of the gate. He'd not returned, and Travis had the security records to prove he'd not been home.

Joshua and Justin sat across from him in his office, their faces worried. Their brother was missing.

Glancing at the picture of Samantha on his desk, he held the phone to his ear as he waited for his brother Tucker to answer.

Of course, Tucker was gone with his wife, Kendra, and his daughter, Nancy Rose, on Kendra's world tour. He was in charge of her security and oversaw it at each venue. There were too many crazies in the world who wanted nothing more than to get to his wife and now his baby girl.

And Kendra Wood was a hot name in Hollywood, known for her acting and singing.

"Hello," his brother said finally answering his phone.

"Hey, I've got a problem here at the ranch and I need your

help," Travis said, leaning back and gazing at his cousins who sat with concerned expressions.

"What's wrong?" Tucker asked, instantly all business.

"Jacob is missing. He's not been seen since Saturday early morning."

"And you're just now calling me? What the hell took you so long?"

Travis took a deep breath; Tucker was right. They needed to watch out for one another. "Just found out myself late yesterday."

"Have you called the police?"

That had been a struggle. And he wasn't certain how Tucker would feel about him contacting them before he spoke to the head of Burnett Security.

"No, we thought it would be better to contact you first," Travis said. "Honestly, we didn't realize he had not come home until late yesterday and then we called his cell phone and started searching for him. I've run out of options, and frankly, I'm worried."

"And?"

"Nothing. His cell phone goes to voice mail."

"What about his truck?"

"Since we haven't talked to the police, we don't know," Travis said.

There were a few moments of silence and then Tucker said, "Let me make some calls. As soon as I know something, I'll let you know. Does anyone have any idea where he was going on Saturday?"

Travis glanced at his cousins. They shook their heads.

"Nope. We don't know what his plans were."

"What if he's out with some girl and doesn't want to be bothered?" Tucker asked.

"Then he should have answered his phone at least once," Travis told his brother.

"True," he said.

That was part of the problem. At the next board meeting, he would discuss with the family the need to check up on one another. Or had Jacob left, hoping to take an unknown trip?

"No one has heard or seen him," Travis said.

Tucker cursed. "Do I need to put a personal GPS system on you guys? We're a very rich family and people would love nothing more than to hold us for ransom. We need to be more careful. You need to communicate with one another and let someone know where you're going."

There was no need to tell Travis this, but the younger Burnetts could use some instruction on accountability.

"Agree," Travis said, thinking of his wife and child. It was so hard to watch them leave without him. Just a drive to the grocery store left him worried until they returned.

Even though he knew the odds were slim that a drunk driver would take a second person from his life, he still fretted.

"Let me know when you find out something," Travis said and disconnected the line. "Is Jacob still riding bulls and going to rodeos?"

The two men glanced at one another and shrugged. "I don't know."

Justin shook his head. "You'd think after his last broken bones, he would be done, but I'm not certain. He could be."

Joshua turned and glared at Justin. "Why didn't you tell me?"

53

"You've been a little busy adjusting to fatherhood, and now you're expecting your second baby."

It was true. Joshua had gone from the Burnetts' playboy to a steady father of a precious little girl. Travis and his wife were watching Baby Sam learn to crawl and say his first words. Travis had never been happier than when he was with Samantha and his son.

Tanner and his wife's adorable little boy Brandon had a precious laugh that his father loved, and so far, Tanner had not returned to having PTSD spells. The Burnetts were getting married and having babies, which their ghostly grandmother was thrilled about.

Only now, Jacob was missing. And that frightened Travis.

"Tucker is right. We need to keep better track of each other. Has anyone let Aunt Rose know? She's going to be fit to be tied if she learns this from the news. And you know once Tucker starts searching, it's going to come out."

Joshua wiped his face with his hand. "I'll tell her."

That was not going to be a fun conversation. Especially when she learned they were not keeping track of one another.

"I'm going to contact the rodeos in the area that were held last Saturday night and see if I can find if he was in one," Justin said. "He has that crazy dream about being a professional bull rider."

Just then Travis's cell phone rang and he grabbed it.

"That was fast. What did you learn?" He put him on speakerphone so Jacob's brothers could hear him.

"The police in Texarkana are worried something's happened to him. Seems his wallet was found on a dead man."

Travis cursed.

"The man was a known druggie and he scored enough

meth on Saturday night that it sent him right on to the pearly gates. If he robbed Jacob, then that could be why and how he scored so much of that killer junk."

The question hung between them and he feared asking.

"Where is Jacob? Where is his truck?"

"That's a good question. I've got some feelers out to find out about his truck. His phone is not pinging its location, so that means it's either turned off or been destroyed. Have Desiree call the credit card companies and put a stop on them. The police said his wallet only contained his license. Whatever cash he had on him is long gone and the credit cards are who knows where."

Travis's heart sank in his chest. "Why would they do this?"

It didn't sound good for Jacob, and Travis needed to alert the family.

"Any number of reasons. My men are working on finding him," Tucker said. "Tell the family just in case we need to prepare for the worst."

Joshua jumped up and began to pace the room.

"No," Justin replied. "He's not dead. I don't believe it."

Travis knew how much it would hurt to learn if one of his brothers had been killed. All they could do was hope and pray that Jacob was somewhere being held hostage or maybe in a hospital unable to speak. It would be hard on everyone if something happened to him.

"I'll give you a call back as soon as I learn more," Tucker said. "My men are all working on finding out what happened to Jacob."

"Thanks," Travis said as he disconnected the call. They were lucky that one of the family had their own security company with connections to law enforcement.

Joshua turned toward the door. "I'll tell Aunt Rose."

Just then his aunt appeared in the doorway. "You'll tell me what? Eugenia has been driving me nuts today, telling me there was something I needed to know. What's going on?"

A scurry of nerves raced down Travis's spine. How had Eugenia known unless Jacob was dead? Like all families, they experienced death, but the last funeral had been for his first wife and child. That one almost killed him.

Thank goodness, now he had Samantha and little Sam. They were his world.

"I was just going to come to your office. Jacob is missing. None of us have seen him since Saturday," Joshua said.

"Saturday?" she exclaimed. "Don't you boys check on one another?"

"Yes, ma'am," Justin told her. "It's been a busy weekend."

"The weekend has been over for several days," she responded, not happy. The woman shook her head, her brows rising on her weathered face. "How in the hell has he been missing since Saturday? That's five days. Has anyone called the police?"

"We contacted Tucker and his men are working on finding him," Travis said.

His aunt seemed to grow older every day and he could see that the thought of one of her nephews missing concerned her.

"They found his wallet on a dead guy. It was empty except for his license. That's how they knew it was his," Joshua told her. "We're really worried."

The older woman sighed.

"If Tucker is searching for him, this is going to hit the press soon. We'll have a whole slew of them outside the gate.

They are to be treated with respect," she said. "They might help us find him if we're kind to them. And if something bad has happened to our sweet boy, then it will be hard to deal with them. Remember how it was when Amanda was killed."

Travis remembered like it was yesterday.

"Call a family meeting," Aunt Rose said. "We need to let everyone know what's going on and to prepare for an onslaught of reporters hanging outside. Our guests need to be told that we expect reporters. And worst of all, we need to be prepared in case we receive bad news."

"Yes, ma'am," Travis said and sent out a text to everyone to meet in the office building. It would be a tight fit, but they had guests playing games in the main building.

This was an emergency blast to them all and they knew to show up right away.

It took fewer than ten minutes for the family to arrive, including his wife and son. When everyone was assembled, except for Emily who was busy preparing the evening meal they would serve their guests, Aunt Rose spoke.

"It's just been brought to my attention that Jacob is missing. The police found his empty wallet. They believe he might have been robbed, but we don't know for certain. Tucker has his men searching for him, and we hope to find out something very soon.

"In the meantime, I'm sure this will soon hit the press and we'll have reporters outside the gates. While we're all worried sick about Jacob, so let's show the press that the Burnett family is a warm, loving family, who protect their own. Be on your best behavior. And let our guests know we are dealing with a family crisis and that reporters are not allowed access onto the property unescorted."

There were murmurs and exclamations of distress as the family gathered around Joshua and Justin.

Travis glanced at his wife, and the look she gave him was like a warm hug. She was his rock. Concern for Jacob filled his mind and he couldn't help but ask the question.

How had Eugenia known? If she knew, then Jacob must be dead.

Oh, how he hoped that wasn't true. He liked Jacob and he didn't want to learn he was gone.

CHAPTER 7

*A*ll night, Hannah lay in bed and thought about how her cash supply was dwindling. No, she wasn't in the red yet, but she had a lot of miles to go and then there was the dreaded trip home.

And everything had to be paid in cash or she'd be discovered.

Oh, how she wished she could just travel the country in her little trailer and paint her way across the United States. She would even enjoy Cowboy going with her and being by her side. Though she wished he would remember his name.

Maybe then he could contribute to paying for their few expenses.

With a sigh, she got out of bed, went to the small window, and glanced at the stars. My goodness, there were so many, and she'd never imagined seeing them on such display until now.

The sky looked filled with a billion dots. A shooting star spiraled to the earth before it flamed out. Was she going to flame out on this trip? It was certainly possible, but she hoped and prayed she would at least make it to Abiquiu.

The sun was just starting to turn pink in the eastern sky and she grabbed her camera and walked out of the camper. She snapped pictures, standing outside in her slinky night-gown. She didn't care because she was taking photos and trying to catch the hues of the early morning sky. So many changing and evolving colors. So many shades of the changing sky.

Suddenly the car door opened and Cowboy stepped out.

"Good morning," he said.

"Good morning," she replied ignoring him as she continued to take photos.

"You're starting awfully early this morning," he said.

She gave him a quick glance. "Do you see that sunrise? Gorgeous. Why are the colors so much more prominent out here in the desert?"

Feeling his stare, she knew he was taking in her state of undress, but he'd get over it. Right now her focus was on nature as the night gave away to day.

Finally, the show came to an end as the sun took over the sky. Turning, she noticed Cowboy at the fire pit.

"Um, that smells delicious," she said.

"It's the last of the coffee," he replied. "I feel so bad that you're paying for everything."

The grin she wanted to contain spread across her face. "Pose nude for me today and we can sell the paintings or even the drawings at the local arts-and-crafts fair. I saw a flyer on the women's bathroom door. It's being held day after tomor-row," she said.

"Whoa, will that give you enough time?"

"Oh, yes," she said with a grin. "As soon as we eat breakfast, we'll find someplace where you can shed everything but your pride."

A grimace crossed his face and she figured he was having second thoughts.

"Come on, we need the cash and I promise I won't show anything other than your derriere," she said. "Though the idea of a picture of you standing out in the desert with your hat positioned in a strategic place might be nice as well."

His brows drew together, and she barely stifled the laugh wanting to burst from her.

"What if someone walks up on us? There are not near the number of trees here like there are back at Pedernales State Park," he said. "I'm not ready to go to jail for indecent exposure."

That wouldn't be good, but she couldn't resist the image of him naked in the desert. She grinned. "I'll tell them that you're getting sun while I sketch you."

"Have you done this before?" he asked.

Laughter escaped from her chest. "Plenty of times in college. I've not had a nude male subject since that time."

Not while living at her parent's home. It would have been the start of World War Three if her father and mother had walked in while she was painting a nude man. Good grief. She'd seen the male parts in college, just never experienced them.

Men didn't really like that her focus was on painting and not them. And she'd never met anyone she wanted to give up painting for. No man had interested her enough to put her paintbrush down.

"We need to get going," she said. "We've got a long day

ahead of us. Plus, I really want to do some sketching of the night skies tonight."

The thought of sitting outside trying to paint in the dark was probably impossible, but they were so beautiful.

"Maybe you should consider getting dressed," he said. "I mean I'm enjoying the scenery, but I'm sure the game warden is not going to be impressed by your nightgown."

With her teasing Cowboy about being naked, she'd forgotten all about still being in her pajamas. "I'll get ready."

"And I'll fix breakfast," he said, grinning at her.

The feel of his eyes on her left her breathless. Why, she didn't understand, but she liked him gazing at her. It was like she was the most beautiful red-haired woman in the world.

Hurrying inside the trailer, she grabbed her well-worn painting clothes, floppy hat, and backpack filled with her paints. She also grabbed a bottle of sunscreen. Neither one of them needed to burn, and she feared under the fall Texas sun, they were going to get toasted.

When she walked outside, the smell of frying eggs and bacon reached her nose.

"That's the last of the eggs and bacon," he said. "We either have to find a farmer or a grocery store."

They were getting low on so many items, and she still had so many miles to cover before she reached her destination. If only she could use her ATM card or credit card or even make a withdrawal from her trust fund. But then they would know her location so that wasn't possible.

She stepped down the stairs of the trailer, her arms loaded.

"I'm ready," she said.

"Breakfast first," he said as he helped remove her painting supplies from her overloaded arms.

His hand brushed against her breast and she gasped.

Turning, he stared at her. "Are you all right?"

"Yes," she said, wondering at her strange reaction to the sensation. Heat had never spiraled through her like that before. It was a pleasant feeling she wanted more of.

Sure, a man in college touched her breasts once, but she'd never reacted like this, like electricity trickling through her body, down to her center. Gazing at him, she couldn't help but wonder how he would look without his clothes.

These drawings, paintings of him, were going to sell like hot cakes. A well-muscled man drawn with just his cowboy hat was a guaranteed sale.

Every day, he'd worn the same clothes, and yet they didn't smell of sweat or body odor, but rather soap. He must be washing them when he took a shower. And the man was fastidious about bathing. Every night, he walked down to the showers.

Taking her by the hand, he led her to the table.

"Time to eat. Then we'll go to wherever you want to draw me. But it has to be off the main path," he said. "I'm not getting naked in front of everyone."

A smile spread across her face and she couldn't help but anticipate seeing him without his clothes. The man's dark hair and rugged good looks left her breathless, so what would his naked chest and thighs look like? What about his very well-rounded booty? Could she draw him without her heart beating out of her chest and her breathing becoming labored? Or even worse, her hands shaking.

They finished breakfast, put the dishes inside the trailer, and then loaded up, even carrying a small cooler filled with cold water and a couple pieces of fruit.

"Ready?" he asked.

Was she ever. Today she would draw him first in her sketchbook and then she would expand. One picture would be in just black and white and she hoped to sell that one at the nearby show. The other would be a painting with him in the backdrop, naked from the rear.

That one she wasn't certain she wanted to sell but knew she might have to. It would be so much fun to have this picture to always remember what the cowboy she'd saved looked like. How he'd gone on this journey with her without knowing his name.

They began the long hike up to the mountains. On a hot fall day, it really was quite a ways, but soon, they were no longer passing people and she knew when she saw the rock outcroppings that she'd found where she wanted to paint.

"Here," she said. "I want you not far from those rock walls."

"You want me to get snake bit," he said.

"No," she said. "But a big strong man like yourself naked near these walls will be quite enticing to women."

Hell, it would be enticing to her. The man had a body she would love to explore. To touch.

Shaking his head, he stared at her. "Are you sure about this?"

"Yes," she replied. "It will give us extra cash when we sell the sketches at the craft fair day after tomorrow. Now, get up there."

With a sigh, he continued on until he was close enough to the walls that she could paint the formations and also include Cowboy.

As she set up her easel with the large sketch pad she'd brought, she couldn't help but notice he was reluctantly removing his clothes. First, he peeled off his cowboy shirt and she'd almost groaned at the sight of his muscles as they rippled along his chest when he moved. Well-sculpted, the sweat from the hike made his skin gleam.

Then he'd removed his boots, but he quickly removed his jeans and underwear before he put his shoes back on. "I'm wearing my boots."

"You do that," she said, thinking that just made the picture perfect. When he turned toward her, he held his hat over his junk and she laughed. If she had time, that would be a sketch for herself. If only he'd drop the hat.

"Are you ready?" he asked, gazing at her with his dark sapphire eyes.

"Yes," she said, thinking her voice sounded breathy.

For the next two hours, she sketched him against the rock formations, his back broad shoulders, narrow waist, and a booty that was so firm, she just wanted to reach out and touch him, but that was not possible.

All morning, she'd sat drawing him, wondering how he would feel, wanting to glide her hands down his back and along his buttocks before she turned him to face her and removed the hat.

But that wasn't going to happen in real life.

The sun was beginning to sink into the western sky when she finally stopped. The painting she could finish at the campground. There were three sketches. One with his hand leaning against the rock formations. One with his hip against the rock wall, his hat on his head, and his neck tilted to where you couldn't see his face. His hand was placed in a strategic place and she'd done her best not to peek, but it had been so hard not to gaze at him.

The third was of him gazing up at the mountain, his back to her and his hat tilted back. They were all good. Damn good, and it was all she could do not to sell them. She wanted to keep them all, but the painting. The painting would go into an art show.

The others she would sell.

After he was dressed, he came over to where she was putting everything away.

"Well?"

"Well what?" she asked.

"I want to see what you did," he replied. "If you're going to objectify my body, I want to see how I look."

She laughed. The man had a sense of humor that when she first met him, she wasn't certain about. But now after traveling together, she really liked the way he made her laugh.

Even with him feeling sore and broken, he made her smile.

She opened the big sketch tablet and showed him what she'd done.

Gazing at her, he grinned. "They're good."

"Yes," she said. "We'll have no problems selling these."

"We won't go to the pokey for pornography, will we?"

"No," she said. "This is art. Beautiful art, and I can't wait to finish the painting."

Pulling her to him, he gazed down into her face and she wanted him to kiss her. All day, she'd been gazing at his rock-solid, naked body, and right now, she needed him to kiss her. She longed to feel his lips on hers.

Would his kiss be soft or demanding? She had to find out.

"I was afraid, but you really did a beautiful job," he said.

Just then a ranger came riding up on a horse.

"It's getting late," he said. "Time to start hiking back to camp unless you plan on spending the night out here."

Damn, the man's timing couldn't have been any worse. She'd wanted that kiss so badly, and she'd been certain he was going to put his lips on hers until the interruption.

But it was for the best.

"We're leaving now," Cowboy told him, stepping back from her.

"Your face looks familiar," the man said, gazing at Cowboy. "I'm not certain where I saw it. Do you have a price on your head?"

"No, sir," Cowboy said.

How did he know that for certain?

"If I get time, I'm going to look and see where I saw your face," he said.

Somebody was searching for him. So why didn't he say anything?

After the man rode off, she gazed at him. "Why didn't you tell him?"

"I don't know. It just felt weird. And I was afraid he'd haul me off, away from you. I don't want us to be separated."

At least not yet. Sooner or later, something would pull them apart. She was certain she knew what too.

Swirling emotions filled her body. If only she knew more about Cowboy. But today, she'd longed for him to kiss her, her body scorching with heat.

This was dangerous. She felt herself drawn toward the flame, and she wanted to experience the fire. To feel the burn.

But, damn, it was impossible and she wanted it so much.

CHAPTER 8

*T*wo days later, the trailer was packed and hooked up to the old SUV. As soon as they sold all the sketches, they were going to leave and drive to the Guadalupe Mountains.

He had mixed emotions about Hannah selling the near-naked portraits of him. While he knew they needed the money, he didn't like the idea of people purchasing his bare backside. It felt strange.

And yet, he had to do something to help their situation. Their supplies were getting low, and it was because she was supporting him. He didn't like that one bit. If only he'd remember who he was so he could get some cash. If he had any.

Standing in the rented booth, he watched as people shopped at the fair. It was a beautiful day to be out and soon they'd be back on the road again.

The Guadalupe Mountains were the last stop before she headed into New Mexico, stopping in Santa Fe, and then proceeding to her painter's home.

The time was coming when he needed to make a decision to stay with her or leave. But he still didn't know who he was and it drove him nuts.

Flashes of memories were becoming more and more frequent, but nothing that would tell him anything useful. He kept seeing a ranch, and he hoped and prayed that was his home, but nothing confirmed his suspicions.

There was still a lot missing from his memories. Especially that time frame just before Hannah found him.

"Are you the cowboy in this picture?" a woman asked him as she gazed at the different sketches that Hannah had created.

"Yes, ma'am," he said.

She made a noise that sounded almost like a growl. "Honey, I know your face. I just can't remember your name."

That made two of them.

"You ride in the rodeo? I was at a rodeo in Texarkana this weekend—" She stopped and stared at him. "I think you were one of those crazy bull riders. My brother rides bulls, even though we keep trying to talk him out of that sport. Yes, they walked you out because you came flying off that bull and landed in the ring really hard. Are you all right?"

What could he say? Had he been riding in the rodeo? It could explain a few of his bruises, but not all of them. And his legs and manly parts had been so sore. Bouncing on the back of a bull could do that to a man.

"I'm fine," he said.

"Well, this seems like much better work," she said. "At least a pencil or a paintbrush won't knock you in the head."

But if he'd been injured riding a bull how had he lost his wallet? His phone?

"Thanks, ma'am," he said and turned away.

Was he a professional bull rider?

So many questions.

"One more and we're out of here and on the road," Hannah said. "We've made almost a thousand dollars this morning. That should help feed us."

Wow, he had no idea those pictures could bring in that much money. She had drawn up more and more of the same ones, so they had extras to sell.

"That woman said she saw you in Texarkana," Hannah said. "That's not too far from where I picked you up."

"Yup," he said, gazing out at the crowd. What if he stayed like this forever?

That was his biggest fear.

"When we stop, maybe you should try to contact the rodeo association and see if you were there that night," she said. "Or even better, contact the Texarkana rodeo and see what they tell you."

He nodded. It would be so good to remember something about himself, but was he really a bull rider?

"When are we leaving?" he asked. "Doesn't look like there's much between here and the next campground."

"The park is two and a half hours from here," she said. "So let's stock up before we leave town."

They had rented a small canopy at the arts-and-crafts fair, and so far, it had paid off as he watched people walking around.

A woman walked up to their booth and stared at Hannah.

"You look like that heiress from New York that is missing," she said, studying Hannah.

Her red hair fell to the front of her face as she gazed at the woman. "An heiress? Really? Then I wouldn't have to paint for a living."

The woman laughed. "True. She's been missing for a least three weeks. Where do you live?"

"Florida, ma'am. That's a ways from New York."

The lady shrugged and gazed at her. "You two could be sisters. Only she had blonde hair."

"You know redheads have all the power."

The woman laughed.

Jacob listened as Hannah tried to convince the woman she was not the same person. Why did it feel like the woman was right and Hannah was trying to brush her off?

"Maybe we are sisters and then I could have a rich inheritance as well. I wouldn't be traveling the country selling my work."

Liar. Jacob could see with his own eyes how much she enjoyed painting. It was in her blood, and she wouldn't give it up for anyone, and she shouldn't have to.

The woman gave a little laugh. "I better move on. My family will be searching for me."

"I've got one last sketch to sell," Hannah said. "You could buy it and tell everyone that you bought it from the missing heiress."

The woman shook her head and walked on.

"People," Hannah said. "If I wasn't that heiress, she didn't want the sketch."

It was true. Five minutes later, they sold the last drawing and he packed up their supplies.

"Let's get out of here," she said. He could tell she was nervous by her rushing around to leave.

Just then the woman who accused her of being the heiress walked up. "You know, I think I'll take that last sketch."

"We just sold it," Hannah told the woman.

It wasn't a lie.

"Oh," she said. "Do you have any others?"

"No, I sold everything I brought," Hannah told her and he knew for a fact she had other sketches and paintings.

Why didn't she want to sell one to this woman? Was it because she'd accused her of being a missing person? And was she that missing person? He didn't think so, but she did appear to be hiding things and he didn't understand why.

And why did she only use cash? Every adult had a credit card or an ATM nowadays. That seemed weird.

"All right," the woman said as Hannah packed things away. "Next time you're here."

Hannah nodded, which surprised him. She was leading the stranger on. They would never return here or so he believed.

Disappointed, the woman walked away.

"You didn't have anything else you could have sold her?"

"No," Hannah said in a sharp, quick tone. "She should have bought it the first time. I think she wanted my signature so she could contact the missing person's report and say *hey I know where your girl is*."

"Are you the missing heiress," he asked suddenly feeling uncertain.

"No," she said with a shrug as she packed things away. "But I'll take her money."

Something about this exchange made him feel wary. He wasn't quite certain she was telling him the truth.

Turning to him, she asked, "Are you ready?"

His arms were filled with her stool and table. She carried the cash box.

"Let's go to the grocery store and then we'll head to the Guadalupe Mountains where we'll spend two days."

Two days were about as long as they stayed in one spot before they moved on. If she was the missing heiress, that could mean people wouldn't have the chance to locate her.

When they reached the SUV and trailer, she unlocked it and quickly put everything away.

"All right," she said. "We're ready to hit the grocery store and then we can head out."

Automatically, he stepped to the driver's side of the SUV. Her brows rose. "You're driving?"

A grin spread across his face. "Why not? We're just going to the store."

When she climbed into the SUV, he saw the same woman who'd questioned Hannah recording them with her phone.

"Let's go," Hannah said. "I don't trust that woman."

"What are you running from?" he asked her.

Swirling around in her seat, she shook her head. "Nothing. But I don't like people who make groundless accusations."

If she was this heiress, it could explain why he didn't believe her family knew where she was.

The SUV passed right by the woman and Hannah turned her face away so the lady couldn't get her image. She was acting strange.

They stopped at a market and he'd never experienced buying groceries like this. It felt intimate like they were a couple, and yet they weren't.

"Do you like orange juice," she asked.

"Yes," he said.

She smiled and put a carton in the buggy.

"What don't you like?" she asked.

"Not much," he replied and wondered how he would know that. But he didn't think he was a picky eater.

Coming around a corner, she stopped and he ran into the back of her. Their bodies came together, his penis pressing against her backside, his chest snug against her back. She turned in his arms.

Her breathing was heavy as she gazed up at him, her emerald eyes sparkling with desire.

His arms naturally went around her. "Sorry. I didn't mean to run over you."

"I'm fine," she said, starring into his eyes. He leaned his mouth down to hers, and then she shook her head and stepped out of his arms.

For a moment, he'd wanted to kiss her so badly, but then she stepped away.

"Let's finish up, so we can get on the road," she said. "Besides, I'm starving after buying all this food. Are we going to eat out or do you want to cook when we get to the camping site?"

Running his finger down her arm, he noticed she shivered.

Things were changing between them and he wasn't certain if that was a good or bad thing. But the woman drove him crazy during the day. He loved to watch her work, and seeing artistry through her eyes was a unique experience.

And yet, he hated that he couldn't tell her who he was. That he couldn't push her against the side of the trailer and let his lips tell her what he was beginning to feel.

How he longed to kiss her. Put his hands on her flesh and show her how she made him crazy.

As they paid for the groceries, he loaded his arms with the bags and they walked out of the store and into the parking lot.

"I'll drive, so we can get set up in the park," she said.

"Yes," he agreed. He still couldn't put a name on any paperwork.

When she pulled out of the parking lot, he gazed at her. What if she was that heiress they were searching for?

"Where about in Florida do you live?" he asked.

She glanced at him, frowning. "Jacksonville, why?"

"Just wondered," he said. Had she ever told him her last name? "What's your last name, Hannah?"

Not looking at him, she said, "Little. Why? Did you believe that woman?"

In some ways he did, but he would never tell Hannah that.

"No, but I realized how little I know about you. We've been concentrating on finding out about me, and I know nothing about you, besides you like to paint."

"What more do you need to know about me? I'm not married. Just a painter, whose family doesn't understand her need to create, traveling to where her idol lived, and wants to paint in the same places she did. It's been a dream of mine since I was in high school."

He nodded. "It's nice to know things about the people you're traveling with."

She glanced at him. "You're right. I'd like to know more about you."

Strange feelings spread through him. "Understand. I would too. Let's hope in time I learn who I am," he said. "But right now, I'm starving. Let's pull over at the next restaurant."

"Agree," she said.

CHAPTER 9

$\mathcal{E}$very time Travis's cell phone rang, he jumped and prepared himself for bad news. This time was no different. Reluctantly, he answered the call.

"What's up," he said as he saw Tucker's number come up on the screen, fearful of what was coming.

"His truck has been chopped up and sold for pieces," he said. "I learned this from one of my snitches. He told me the truck is gone. Jacob will need to buy another one."

Travis cursed.

"I don't give a damn about the truck. We'll turn it in to the insurance company and say it's a total loss. But where is Jacob?"

What had his brother found out about him?

There was a heavy sigh on the phone.

"Jacob is still missing," he said. "No body has been found, which is a good thing. My lead investigator found out he rode in a rodeo in Texarkana on Saturday night. He was hurt, but they let him drive off. The medic tried to convince him to go to the hospital, but he refused. He told them he was going home."

The kid was hurt, but he attempted to drive home that night. Not good.

"Have you checked the hospitals?"

"Of course," Tucker said. "Nothing."

There was silence on the phone.

"Good grief, I hope the kid is all right," Travis said. "Somewhere on the way home, he must have been robbed. The druggie who died, where was he from?"

"Linden, Texas," Tucker said. "I spoke to his friend and he told me they were home by midnight that night. That they found Jacob's wallet outside a country and western bar. Jacob is not a barhopping guy."

It was true, Jacob was more a man who liked to stay home. They teased him that he was never going to marry because he didn't go out and meet women. But he didn't seem to care.

"That's a lie," Travis told his brother. "That doesn't sound like Jacob. Did you check the man's background?"

Tucker laughed. "He spent two years in the pen for robbery."

"There you go," Travis replied. "Did he stop for gas somewhere? Have you checked his credit card transactions?"

"No, but that's a good idea. If he stopped for gas and was robbed, that could be a good place to start looking for him," Tucker said. "I'll get one of my men on that right away."

Travis sighed. This had never happened to any of them, and it wasn't pleasant, and frankly, he was worried. If Jacob was all right, he would be home. He would have called and said he needed help.

"There is a report of a lady saying she saw him in the Davis

Mountains with a woman, but I'm not certain I believe that's true. Who would this woman be? And what is he doing in the Davis Mountains?"

That didn't make any sense.

"When did you get that report?"

"Today," he said. "One of the bull riders said his sister saw him there and said he acted strange. He knew about Jacob missing and called me. But why would he be there?"

It was all strange. "Well, at least we're hearing reports of him being alive. I've feared the worst. He can explain the reason for him being there when we find him."

"I have two men who landed in Austin and they're headed in that direction. I'm just hoping he's still there."

No matter what, he hoped Jacob was safe. Why would he not be home?

"Do you think it's him?"

"Don't know," Tucker said. "But why wouldn't he have found a way to let us know he was okay? Why wouldn't he need help sincc hc's been robbed?"

It was all a big confusing mystery.

"I'll let the others know, but I think you should call Joshua and Justin and tell them about their brother. I'll let Aunt Rose know. We have about ten reporters hanging around outside the main entrance," Travis told his brother. "Once they learn he's alive, they'll want to talk to him. Ask him what happened."

Even more reporters would show up, and then they would indeed have a circus on their hands. But first, they needed to find out if this was Jacob, and if so, why hadn't he called. Something had to be wrong for him not to contact them. The man was a good guy and wasn't one for doing this kind of nonsense.

"Do I need to send a security detail there?"

For a moment, it was tempting to let Tucker handle the reporters outside, but he'd better check with Aunt Rose first. The woman didn't like being left out of any major decisions. She ran this operation and she made certain they all understood she was in charge.

"No, I think we can handle them," Travis told his younger brother. "How's the tour?"

He laughed. "Let's see, we're only on the second city, and already, I've fired two men for working for the scandal rags. The baby has been sick and my wife loves this life. She loves performing, but I worry about her."

Travis smiled. "Understand, little brother, but you love her, so you'll do just fine protecting her."

A noise erupted in the background. "Hang on a moment."

Travis heard a crackling noise.

Tucker came back on the line. "They were spotted this morning at a craft fair in Fort Davis, Texas. My men are racing there now."

"They?"

"Yes, a woman is with him," he said.

"Hmm, that's not what I expected to hear."

Why would Jacob sneak off with a woman and not tell anyone? What was he doing after being robbed? None of this made a lick of sense. But it sounded like he was still alive and thank God for that. The thought of planning a funeral for one of his cousins left him cringing. He'd already done that more than once and he wasn't up to doing it again anytime soon.

"Let's hope he has a good reason for why he's disappeared without telling any of us."

Travis chuckled. "Oh, I think Aunt Rose will have him cleaning pigpens for a while."

"That sucks for him," Tucker said. "If I hear anything else, I'll let you know. I think we're getting close to finding him."

"I hope so," Travis said. "I want him to be all right."

"Me too," Tucker said.

They disconnected the line and Travis rose from his chair and went in search of Aunt Rose. She wanted to be kept up to date with what was happening with Jacob. If they were close to finding him, then she needed to know before the press found out.

CHAPTER 10

*V*an Horn was a small town with only four red lights, several hotels, and a diner that looked like it was built in the '50s.

Breakfast had been hours ago and they were both hungry but she was anxious to get to the national park.

Hannah pulled the SUV and trailer into the parking lot of the older building that said *homemade food* out front. She glanced around at the assortment of trucks, pickups, and cars and knew this was a very small town where the locals probably hung out at the cafe.

The place was a weird spot in the road where ranchers and people going to and from Mexico seemed to intersect. Only thirty miles from the Mexican border, she'd read the little city was in one of the most active corridors for illegal drug smuggling.

"Is this all right? I'm starving," she said. "You know we're in a dangerous area."

"Yeah," Cowboy said as he exited the SUV looking around the parking lot. "We'll be careful. If we're not comfortable when we walk in, we'll leave. Let's get a bite then we can drive to the national park and set up camp."

"Sounds good," she said, locking the car.

The place wasn't a dive, but rather a homestyle restaurant that would either have great food or you could get food poisoning. At the moment, she was ready to take her chances.

A smile spread across her face. She felt this urge to reach out and grab his hand as they walked across the parking lot, but she didn't. There was an easiness between them that she really liked. Not the stuffiness of the previous men she'd dated. Not like Maxwell, who never took her hand.

But Cowboy and she weren't dating. They were just two people on the road together. Two people who needed to consider going on to New Mexico quickly. She felt uneasy in this area. It didn't feel safe, and she hadn't felt that way before now. Not in any of the parks she'd stayed in.

When they entered the diner, a television was up on the wall showing the national news.

They sank at a table and soon the waitress came over and handed them a couple of menus.

They stared at the selections.

"I don't see cowboy goulash on here," she teased.

"I don't see fried crappie or tacos," he said. "You have to admit, the food we've been eating is pretty good."

"Yes, but we're not cooking tonight," she replied. At the grocery store, she'd restocked the little camper and they should be set for at least a couple of weeks.

In two weeks, she had to be back in New York. And one month later…she pushed the thought out of her mind. She was on her dream trip, and for the last week, she'd been sharing it with Cowboy.

"I think I'm going to get the chicken fried steak," he said.

"Me too. That sounds so good." She shut her menu.

The waitress returned and they placed their order.

The diner was filled with locals. Mainly ranchers and oil field workers and a few city folk who must've worked in town. They were the oddballs in the cafe, though Cowboy was wearing his hat.

It had been a long day and she was beginning to tire. Maybe that was why she felt apprehensive as she stared at the locals filling the cafe. None of them seemed to pay them any attention and she was just being paranoid.

"What are you painting in the Guadalupe Mountains?"

"The scenery," she said. "I also would like to get over to Carlsbad Caverns. Maybe paint the bats coming out in the evening."

He nodded and smiled. "That's a really interesting thing to witness. All the bats coming out at once. It's shocking that there are so many. I don't know how you could separate them. It's like one big black cloud with wings."

"So you've been there," she said.

"Yes, but don't ask me any questions. All I know is that I visited there as a boy. I remember sitting on the benches and staring at the opening."

With a sigh, she wondered how long it was going to take before his memory returned. "Tomorrow, it will have been a week since I picked you up."

"Yes," he said. "I would have thought my memory would've returned by now. But so far only glimpses. I just hope and pray it doesn't stay this way. When I least expect it, I get flashes of my life before, but not enough information to let me know who I am."

"You should still see a doctor. I thought within a couple of days, you'd remember what happened to you," she said. She truly believed he couldn't remember because he got so frustrated recalling only bits and pieces.

The noise of dishes clinked in the restaurant and she noticed their waitress was on the phone. She kept staring at them.

"Have you decided if you're going to go on to New Mexico with me?"

She wasn't ready for him to leave. Maybe she would feel different once she found out who he was, but right now, she wanted him to stay. She enjoyed his company and even his fishing. There was something happening between them, and if he left, she would be so disappointed.

And yet, she had secrets of her own she had not told him. Today, she'd been shocked when that woman recognized her. How in the hell had someone from Texas learned that she was missing?

And she wanted to do more nude sketches of him, though she wasn't certain he would agree. She'd even agree to do sketches of him with his clothes on.

For the last week, he'd spent every night sleeping in the back of her SUV. He'd never once tried to press himself on her and that was something. At first, she'd been a little afraid of him, but now she truly believed he was a good man who had just run into some trouble.

But she also knew that if pictures of her with a man were seen on the internet or by the men she was certain her father had searching for her, she'd be in so much crap. Sometimes she didn't care because maybe then her father would leave her alone. Though she couldn't imagine living without her family.

They were his leverage against her and he used them to get her to do what he wanted.

But now he'd gone too far.

The waitress brought their food and set it in front of them.

Hungrily, they both dug in.

He grinned at her when she moaned. "You like chicken fried steak? That's a southern food."

"I love chicken fried steak," she said. "I don't care that it's a southern food."

"I didn't think they fixed it up in New York City," he said.

She stopped and stared at him. Was he trying to trick her into saying she was from New York? Well, it wouldn't work.

"No, but there are places in Florida that fix it very well," she said.

"So you're from New York," he said and she could see that he thought he'd gotten one past her.

"Not unless Jacksonville is now in the middle of the city," she said. "You're trying to trick me and it didn't work."

A shrug came from his shoulders. "Honey, right now, I don't care where you're from. We're eating great food and even the back seat of your old SUV is not going to stop me from sleeping tonight."

He'd called her honey and that made her heart flip.

Maybe she should feel sorry that he was sleeping back there, but he wasn't going to snuggle up with her in the trailer. Though the feel of those hard muscles wrapped around her was tempting.

The waitress brought them a dessert menu. "On the house tonight. Pick which one you want."

"Thanks," Hannah said.

"On the house," Cowboy said. "That's odd."

"Maybe it's a special they run," she said, glancing at the selections. Dessert sounded so wonderful.

Were the people in the diner staring at them? Whispers seemed to be going around the room and people were gazing at them like they were an oddity. What the hell was going on?

They ordered chocolate cake and coffee.

It would be dark by the time they made it up the road to the national park and were assigned their campground, but it had been so worth stopping here and having a full meal.

She reached across the table and took his hand. A shimmery heat spread through her at his touch and she had to squeeze her lips together to keep from gasping. "Thank you for posing for me. If you hadn't, we would not be here eating."

"You're welcome," he said, smiling. "Glad I could help with our finances in some small way."

"I thought there for a little while, I was going to have to beat the women off you," she said. "That one girl didn't want to give up. Especially, when she realized you were the cowboy in the sketch."

A blush spread across his face. "Yes, she was determined."

The waitress brought the cake over and they eat the scrumptious dessert. There was a sudden loud murmur in the restaurant and she felt like all eyes were on them. Glancing up at the television, she saw his face on the screen.

With a whimper, she knew why everyone was talking about them.

"Cowboy, turn around and look at the television."

An old picture of him was on the screen. He whirled around and she heard him gasp.

"Jacob Burnett," she said. "Your name is Jacob Burnett."

When he turned back around, he smiled at her before

turning back to the television. He laughed. "Yes, I'm part owner of the Burnett Ranch. It says my family is searching for me. There is a reward being offered."

"Does any of this sound familiar?" she asked.

"Yes," he said with a gasp. "It's all starting to come back."

Putting his hands to his head, he gripped his forehead like it was hurting and she suddenly grew worried.

"Are you all right?"

"Yeah," he said. "Seeing the television made it all come rushing back. My past, right up to the time I was robbed."

"Tell me," she said softly as she reached out and touched his arm, afraid of what he was going to say to her.

"I went to a rodeo on Saturday night where a bull took me out of the competition. I hit my head pretty bad when he knocked me off, and they wouldn't let me continue. I fell asleep in my truck and when I woke up, it was late. I wanted to get home, so I took off toward the ranch, which was about a four-hour drive."

A shiver went through him. "It was late. But I stopped to fill up with gas. That's when they blocked me in at the gas station. Before I could unlock my gun, they attacked me."

Listening to him, she watched his facial expression as the memories seemed to come flooding back.

"My truck. They must have stolen my wallet, my phone, my truck, everything from me."

Why they hadn't killed him, she didn't know. Or maybe they tried and were interrupted. But thank God, he was still alive.

"We need to let your family know you're alive," she said.

"Agreed," he said. "They probably have a phone here I can use."

Just then the door to the diner swung open and four big burly guys walked inside. With disbelief, she watched as they marched straight to them.

"Jacob Burnett," the man asked.

"I think so," Cowboy said.

"We're with Burnett Security. Your family is worried sick about you. We're here to escort you home," he said.

Jacob glanced at her. Their time together was over. He would be leaving with these men.

"Hannah, come with me," he said. "The ranch isn't far from here and I could pay you back what I owe you. You could meet my family. You're my savior and I'm not ready to cut the cord with you. Stay for just a day or two. I'll even pose nude again for you," he said with a smile.

The thought of making more sketches of him was tempting. And she wasn't ready to part from him just yet either. But this would take her off course. The Guadalupe Mountains had not been her favorite, something about the area was scary.

Maybe there were scenery pictures at his ranch she could paint.

"Please, Hannah, come with me," he said, reaching out and taking her hand.

Everyone in the diner watched them.

The men in the black suits had surrounded their table. She and Jacob were not going to get away from them.

"Sir, your family has thought you were dead for almost a week," the man said.

"I'm sorry, I didn't know who I was until just now when we saw the missing person's report on television," he said. "My brain is still foggy."

Would it be safe for Hannah to travel to the Burnett Ranch

or would that put a target on her back? She could be endangering her entire trip by going off with Jacob. But something was happening between them, and while she knew it was impossible, she didn't want to leave him. Not yet. She wasn't ready to say good-bye.

If she were free to date, he would be the type of man she would want.

"Please, Hannah," he said. "I can't let you go yet."

Still holding her hand, he gave it a squeeze and desire flowed through her.

Leaning in toward him, she nodded. "I'll go, but I don't want anyone to know where I'm at. You've got to keep me hidden."

A grin spread across his face. "I'll do my best. You can paint the Burnett Ranch."

Standing, she pulled out money and left it on the table for the waitress, and Jacob put his hand on the small of her back as he escorted her out of the building.

The men in black suits filed in line behind them. When they reached her car, the man who seemed to be in charge grunted at them.

"Two cars will be in front of you and two behind you," he said. "You stay safely in the middle."

She handed him the keys.

"You know the way. You drive," she said.

He laughed. "No, I don't know the way, but I can follow them. We're going home, Hannah. I can't wait to introduce you to the family. They're going to love you."

Nerves suddenly gripped her as she climbed into the passenger seat. What the hell was she doing, taking a chance on not following her plan? Was she risking her dream to help get the cowboy home where he belonged?

And wasn't it going to be even harder to leave him once she saw where he lived and met his family? Wasn't leaving him behind going to be tough regardless of when it happened?

She had an obligation to her family, and no matter how much she hated it, she had no choice. How would Jacob feel when he learned the truth?

With a sigh, she glanced out the window as they pulled out behind the two security cars. What was she doing?

CHAPTER 11

*A*ll the way back to the ranch, Jacob told her about his family. The memories came rushing back and filled him with so much joy. Not knowing who he was drove him crazy.

There was a lightness in his soul and he wanted to reach over and grab Hannah's hand. She'd been his salvation and played such an important part in taking care of him. And now that he knew he was free and single, he wanted to show her how much she affected him.

If possible, he wanted what was happening between the two of them to grow.

It would be so good to get home and change out of these clothes. These were going in the trash. There was no rescuing them, no matter how much soap he'd used on them.

When the men said Burnett Security, he'd known that Tucker's men had been searching for him. Tears stung his eyes at the thought of his family trying to find him when he didn't know who or where he was.

"My cousin, Tucker Burnett owns a security company and that's who is traveling with us," he said.

"For a moment there, I thought they were mafia and even considered your family might be a part of them."

He laughed. "Oh no, my family is a bunch of ranchers. We've owned the same ranch for over one hundred years. We even supposedly have a family ghost on the property, though I've not met her."

"That's interesting. I wonder if she would let me paint her," she said, teasing.

"Hannah, I have to tell you thank you. You took me in and have helped me so much this past week. Most people would not have taken a chance on a man who couldn't tell you his name. Thank you."

Any smart woman wouldn't have done what she'd done, but fate had different plans for them.

Turning to gaze at him, he could see she had tears in her eyes. "I was a little afraid of you, at first."

Laughter bubbled up from his chest that felt so much lighter now that he knew who he was.

"Oh yes, I remember that Taser you threatened me with," he said, grinning. "Would you have used it on me?"

"Yes," she said.

It was dark and it would be almost ten o'clock when they arrived at the ranch. But tonight he would sleep in his bed, not the back seat of her car.

"My ranch also has a dude ranch. We have guests who come and stay a week and learn what living on a ranch is like. It's a big business for us," he said.

Whirling toward him, her eyes widened. "Really? Jacob, for the love of God, I need for no one to know I'm there."

It was strange that she wanted to remain so anonymous. Why?

"Who are you hiding from?"

"My family," she said. "Unlike you, I don't want them to know where I am. Not for a while. They will make my life a living hell. They will end my dream trip and never let me out of their sight again."

That seemed preposterous that he wanted his family to find him and she wanted nothing to do with hers. He couldn't imagine their situations being so reversed. No, she had to be wrong about them making her life hell.

"Have you tried making up with them?"

Even in the darkness of the car, he could see the distress on her face. "There is nothing to make up about. They want things from me that I'm having a hard time accepting. I can't do this. If they learn I'm here, it won't be pretty. Maybe I should leave in the morning," she said.

"No," he said suddenly fearful. "Stay a few days. I'll do my best to make certain no one knows you're there."

Turning, she stared at him. "I want to stay, but my dreams are in Abiquiu. That's where I'm destined to paint."

Yes, he knew she wanted to go there, but he still wasn't ready to separate from her, not yet. Not until he could go with her. The thought of her driving up there by herself made him nervous.

It would have been hard to have left her in Van Horn. A woman staying alone in the national park without a cell phone and with drug smugglers close by. Just no. Now that he knew where they were, he could not have left her there alone.

She took a deep breath and he knew she was anxious. He'd known since that woman approached them.

Suddenly the big gates were there in front of them and they were surrounded by reporters. "Get down."

"What?"

"Reporters are at the gates. Get down," he said, trying to protect her. He'd been questioning if she could be that heiress the woman accused her of being.

She undid her seat belt and slid to the floor where she crouched, hiding her face.

Slowly he pulled through the gates, the flash of iPhone cameras and even the big fancy flashbulbs went off as he drove onto the grounds. He watched in the rearview mirror as the two black cars behind him drove in and then two men got out and shut the gates, pushing the reporters out.

If Hannah was this afraid, how was he going to keep his family from not telling the world she was here with him? And what about his cousin Tucker? The man would be investigating her if he said anything, and maybe even if he didn't.

Suddenly, there was family running toward the cars and his heart swelled with emotion. Even his Aunt Rose was hobbling out of the big house and making her way toward them.

The door was yanked open and Joshua pulled him out and into a big hug. "Damn man, you scared the hell out of us. Where have you been?"

"Wasn't too great for me either. Easy on the ribs, they're still broken."

Justin pushed his brother out of the way. "Next time you leave the ranch, we're putting a GPS on you. We thought you were dead."

His eyes teared with love for the people who worried about him. Wouldn't Hannah's family be the same?

It felt so good to be back among the people he loved.

"I almost was," he said. "Hannah rescued me."

"Hannah?" Aunt Rose said as she walked up glancing around. "I don't see anyone."

He leaned into the car. "It's all right. The reporters are gone. You can come out now."

They all turned and stared as the red-haired woman curled out of the floorboard and then opened the door and stepped out.

She came over to his side and they all stared at her.

"Everyone, this is Hannah," he said, realizing he couldn't remember her last name. If she told him, he'd forgotten, and after their discussion, he wondered if she would tell her real name.

"Christenson," she said. "Hannah Christenson."

"Nice to meet you, Hannah," Aunt Rose said. "We're so thankful you saved our boy."

Oh, great, she'd called him a boy in front of the woman he really wanted to get to know better. The woman he wanted to feel close to his side. The woman who made his skin burn and tingle and his insides flow like hot lava.

He'd been aching for days to pull her against him and kiss those beautiful full lips of hers, and now he could.

Hannah nodded. "All I did was pick him up when he was walking down the middle of the road at three in the morning."

Travis stepped forward and nodded at Hannah. "Thank goodness you did or he could be dead. Tucker said that you're going to need a new truck. Yours was stripped and sold for parts."

Shaking his head, Jacob sighed. "I liked that truck. I guess my phone, wallet, and my gun are gone."

"Your wallet was found on a dead guy," he told him.

"What?"

"Seems the jackass took the money and bought meth. Enough that he's no longer here to serve time."

Jacob wondered if it was the guy who appeared to be the leader and who had struck him, including the blow to the back of his head.

"Come on, let's go sit in the pavilion and you can tell us what happened," Aunt Rose said. "I'm too old to be standing outside this late at night."

"I'll serve coffee," Emily, Tanner's wife, said.

"I'll help you," Desiree, his cousin, said following her.

For the next hour, Jacob sat surrounded by his family and told them what happened with Hannah speaking up occasionally and telling them things he'd forgotten.

It felt so good to be home and to finally remember everything about his life. The good, the bad, and even the ugly.

"I'm glad I didn't take my horse with me to the rodeo," he said. "I'd be missing my favorite mare, and those assholes don't deserve her."

Tanner shook his head. "You'd be dead because you would have fought them over that horse."

It was true. As it was, he almost died anyway.

Aunt Rose took Hannah by the hand. "Thank you, dear. If you hadn't picked him up, I fear what might have happened to him. And you, stubborn one, are to go see Dr. Mason in the morning. I'll call him and tell him that you are to be examined from top to bottom. Why didn't you go to a hospital?"

Joshua and Justin glanced at him. They knew why. The memories of their mother dying there were more than they could bear. No, she hadn't been a great mother, but no one deserved to die of breast cancer, and hers had been a long, drawn-out affair. Every time he walked into a hospital, he remembered her death.

"He refused to," Hannah said. "I tried to get him to go several times, but he wouldn't let me take him."

Aunt Rose stood. "It's after midnight and work will go on as usual tomorrow, so we should all get to bed. Jacob, I'm so happy you're all right. But the next time you leave this ranch without telling someone where you're going, you'll get a year of pigpen cleaning duties."

There was a snicker from everyone in the family. Pigpen cleaning was the worst job on the ranch and they all had gotten to experience it at one time or another. That was Aunt Rose's punishment and you never wanted to receive that from her.

"If I wasn't so damn glad to see you, you'd have at least a month of pigpen cleaning, even now, but this time, I just can't," she said. "Miss Hannah, where will you be sleeping?"

"In my trailer," she said, wondering why the old woman was asking, and then it dawned on her. "No, we haven't slept together. Jacob stayed in the back of the SUV and I slept in the trailer with the door locked."

"Smart woman," Aunt Rose said with a chuckle. "Now, excuse me, everyone, it's way past my bedtime."

Aunt Rose hugged Jacob one last time and then walked out the door, her cane thumping.

Travis jumped up. "I'll escort her back to the main house to make certain she doesn't fall in the dark."

"Good idea," Tanner said. "Tucker is going to call you in the morning. Tonight, his wife was giving a concert and he was busy making certain she stayed safe. But tomorrow morning, he said he wanted to speak to you."

"Thanks, Tanner," he said. "I'm eager to hear what he learned about that group that robbed me."

Jacob was tired. It had been a long emotional day, and he was ready to fall asleep in his own bed with his mind intact.

Standing, he walked over to Hannah. "Let's go set up your camper and then I'm going to bed."

The whole family looked at them and smiled. The smell of lavender filled the air. Where was that coming from?

"Eugenia's here," he heard someone say. The ghost? No...

Suddenly an old woman shimmered before him. Was he losing his mind again? No, he didn't believe in ghosts, not even Eugenia.

"Jacob, I'm so happy you're safe," she said. "And Hannah, welcome to the family. You two are such a cute couple. You're going to give me such wonderful grandbabies."

He felt Hannah tense beside him.

And just like that, the vision disappeared.

Everyone laughed.

Several of the women came over to Hannah. "You're about to experience Eugenia's matchmaking."

"Don't fight it. It won't do you any good," Samantha, Travis's wife said. "She's really very sweet, but she's a tad stubborn too."

"I heard that," Eugenia said like a voice from the great beyond, "When are you going to tell everyone you're expecting again?"

Samantha gasped. "Not until it's confirmed."

Travis walked back into the room. "What's going on?"

"Eugenia just told everyone I'm pregnant again," Samantha said, laughing. "We were waiting until we knew for certain."

Travis kissed his wife on the lips. "We're happy. Our family is growing and we can't wait for baby number two to arrive."

Jacob glanced at Hannah. "I warned you about Eugenia, but that's the first time I've ever seen her."

"And it won't be the last," Travis said with a grin.

"Get ready, little brother, I think you're about to be matched," Joshua said.

He glanced at Hannah and her face was drawn into a frown. Maybe she wasn't having the same feelings for him as he was for her. Maybe she didn't want them to become a couple now that all obstacles were cleared for him. Maybe she didn't like his family.

After all, she didn't like her own clan.

CHAPTER 12

*A*s Jacob and she walked to her SUV and trailer, he took hold of her hand. The feel of his palm against hers sent a shiver through her as heat pooled in her womanly areas. It felt so good, so right, and yet she couldn't. But for just this moment, she was going to enjoy the feel of his hand against hers.

Didn't she deserve a little happiness before she had to sacrifice herself? Didn't she deserve this time?

Soon, she would have to go and that would mean leaving Jacob behind for good. But for now, she was going to indulge herself with the touch. She was going to let him kiss her if he wanted.

"Why don't you spend the night at my house," he said. "You would have your own bedroom and bathroom. I promise I won't disturb you, and in the morning, you could even do the laundry you said you needed to do."

That was a tempting offer. A real bed with a bathroom and a bathtub. But if her father learned she'd slept in a man's home, she'd be in so much trouble.

Wait. Why had she been so worried about a man who had no heart? Screw him. She deserved one night of pampered pleasure. These were her memories and she wanted to make as many with Jacob as she could to last her a lifetime.

"All right," she said. "But nothing else."

A grin spread across his face and he continued to hold her hand. "Let's pull your car down to my house and then you can get what you need out of the trailer."

Ten minutes later, Jacob opened the door to his home and turned on the lights. It was a nice place for a single man. A large space with a fireplace, big screen television, and leather sofa in the living room. A kitchen with a dinette table sat on the other side of the room and then there was a hallway off the living room that went to his bedroom.

"You're going to sleep here in the guest room," he said carrying her suitcase down the opposite hall. Hopefully, he would not get any ideas about traipsing to her room. As much as she hated it, she was a virgin and she'd remain one until she said her vows.

She felt awkward, but she wanted to be here with Jacob. In his home. He made her feel safe and secure, and she'd never experienced that with a man.

Being with him was easy and they had fun together, even in the worst of times.

"In the morning, I'll fix us breakfast and then I'll have to go to work. They'll want me to get back to the cattle."

"No," she said. "Your aunt said you were to be checked out by Dr. Mason and I gather she has a lot of pull in this place."

He grinned at her. "You noticed that, did you?"

"Yes, you're lucky to have someone like her," she said.

"She's in charge. Besides, you really need to be checked out by a doctor."

"Aunt Rose is almost eighty and is hell on wheels if things aren't done like she wants them. This ranch is a full-time job for her. The rest of us sit on the board of directors, but she is the leader and nothing gets by her."

The older woman had a commanding presence and Hannah admired her. The entire family was one that seemed to happen only in movies. They were certainly a lot different from her own group. But then this family leader was not a man who let things get out of control and needed to be reined in.

She walked into the guest room. It was very nice, and while it didn't have the view like her room back in New York, it was still the perfect guest suite. A large queen bed that looked so inviting sat in the middle of the room and a door led off to a large private bathroom.

"There should be towels in the guest bath, soap, shampoo, anything you might need. If not, come and get me," he said. "Or I could stay and wash your back."

She grinned. Before now, Jacob had not shown much interest in her, but still, the last few days, she'd felt something building between them.

He set her suitcase down and walked over to her. "You've taken care of me for the last week, now it's my turn to take care of you."

That was an odd statement. "I don't think I took care of you. I was just there in case you needed me."

"And I did, I needed you," he said, putting his hands on her arms and drawing her against his chest. It felt good to be held by him. A feeling of being wanted and desired overwhelmed her. Being in his arms felt right, like this was where she belonged.

If only that were possible.

"If I remember right, there was one day you drove so I could rest," she said against his chest. No one had ever cared for her like he did by making certain she felt better and taking away her burdens. The man had even cooked her dinner that night.

"Yeah, but that was different. Tomorrow morning after I go to the doctor, I'm going to make certain your trailer and SUV are all checked out. I think the brakes might be going bad."

Knowing she would be leaving, he was going to make certain she was safe on the road. No one cared about her like that.

She grinned at him. "You're a cowboy, not a mechanic."

"I can do both," he said.

"You know I can't stay long," she said. "I need to reach Abiquiu before…"

She'd almost said *before she got caught*. There was so much she should tell him, but she feared his reaction. Hell, she hated her own reaction.

And now she dreaded somehow she'd be found.

"Let's just take things one day at a time," he said. "Let's just wait and see before you take off."

That was the problem. She didn't have days to take it easy. But at least she could relax tonight.

"All right," she said. "Now get out of here. There is a big tub in that bathroom and I intend to check it out."

"Do you need my help?" he asked. "I'm really good with a washrag."

She smiled. "No."

He pulled back and gazed down at her, a serious expression on his face, but his sapphire eyes were filled with passion for her. Her heart slammed into her chest and she wanted him kissing her, touching her.

In one week, they had shared a lot and grown close, and it would have to last her a lifetime.

"Hannah, I've wanted to do this for a long time, but I waited until I knew I wasn't tied to anyone. It would have been wrong for me to kiss you if there was someone else in my life. Now that I know I'm free, I can't wait another second."

His mouth came down on hers and she leaned into his kiss. Oh, how she wanted this as much as him, but there were obstacles preventing her from accepting the feelings that were growing for him. Feelings she wanted to give in to but couldn't. Feelings that could destroy her.

She let the kiss continue, knowing it was wrong, but unable to stop herself from enjoying the feel of his lips as they consumed hers. He smelled like leather and soap, and she breathed deeply of his essence.

Finally, she placed her hand between them and broke the kiss. Their breathing was quick and her body responded to him. Heat flowed straight to her center.

Why now? Why?

"Goodnight, Jacob," she said as she turned him and pushed him out the door.

"Goodnight, Hannah. Damn, but you're a good kisser. Didn't you feel that? The passion between us, the heat, the— how is a man supposed to go to sleep after that kiss?"

She laughed and closed the door.

"Just like a woman," he huffed playfully, "kiss a man and then close the door on him."

"Just like a man to tempt a woman and then walk away," she responded.

Suddenly the door opened. "I'm not walking away."

Laughing, she shook her head. "Goodnight, Jacob. Sweet dreams."

Sighing, he closed the door. "Of you, Hannah. Of you."

A sob rose up in her throat.

Closing her eyes, she fought the tears that filled her lids. If only she could promise him the rest of her life, but she couldn't.

Here was a sweet man, who had treated her so well and protected her when he'd had so much to worry about himself. She'd seen him at his worst, and she thought he would be even better at his best. His family was filled with love for one another and she could tell they all wanted everyone to be happy and safe and here in the family circle.

Their bond wasn't about how one member could increase their wealth and stability by sacrificing herself. They genuinely cared for one another.

Tears spilled down her cheeks, her pain gripping her.

The urge to paint almost overwhelmed her. She wanted to paint Jacob again. But this time, she wanted him clothed and gazing out at the land he loved. This time, she wanted to capture the man he was. His gentle spirit, his love, and the way he cared about his family.

This was the type of man she'd always wanted to marry. But that was not meant to happen.

Maybe she could capture the man on her canvas and hold

him close to her heart even though they would always be miles apart.

Shedding her clothes, she filled the tub with bath spirits and crawled in. It felt so good to soak and let the worries slip away. A couple more weeks and then she would be forced to return and give herself up.

With a sigh, she closed her eyes and did her best to think of her paintings, of what she wanted to paint next. Anything to keep her mind off the future.

The smell of lavender filled the room and suddenly the ghost appeared in front of her.

"Are you in love with my grandson?"

Stunned, she stared at the woman. "Jacob is a wonderful man. I could very easily fall in love with him, but I can't. I won't let myself."

The woman frowned at her, her ghostly appearance twinkling.

"Why not? You'd be part of the Burnett family. We take care of those we love," she said. "It would be a great honor if you were to join us. I think you love him."

Oh, how she would love to be a part of a family like this, but her own family needed her, and as much as she hated what they were demanding, she would do it for them.

"I'd be the luckiest woman alive to be able to be with Jacob. He's a great man. But my own family has made it very hard for me and I can't be with him without destroying them."

The woman shook her head vehemently. "No. Tell me now why you can't be with him. I need to understand."

What was wrong with her? She was talking to a ghost while she was naked in the bathtub.

Shaking her head, she sighed. "I just can't be with him."

"Family is the most important thing. And our family watches out for one another. That's why we all knew that something was wrong when Jacob didn't come back. Did you keep him?"

"No, I rescued him," she said. "Now, if you'll excuse me, it's time I crawl into bed. I can't believe I'm talking to a ghost. I need to get some rest to clear my head."

The woman cackled. "Oh, dear, tomorrow you need to speak to Desiree or Samantha or Emily. They can tell you all about me and how I brought them together with their husbands. Whatever this problem is, dear, you need to tell me and I'll get it fixed. You are my choice for Jacob and I know you're his."

Was that true? Yes, she'd enjoyed his kiss tonight and she'd been gazing at his body all week long thinking what a handsome man he was. He was kind and loyal and a good guy. And there was plenty of sexual fire between them. But they could not be together.

"Goodnight, Eugenia," she said, standing in the tub. She reached for a towel just as the woman dissipated. Could she sleep in a home where a ghost was present? Did the woman not understand that this situation was not within her control?

Hell, it was the very reason she'd left New York. At least for a little while, and then she would return and do her daughterly duty, even if it killed her.

And right now, it was looking like it might be the death of her yet.

CHAPTER 13

*E*arly the next morning, the phone rang before Jacob was out of bed. Rolling over, he glanced at the clock and picked up the landline. Odd that someone was calling him at the house number and then he remembered. He didn't have a cell phone any longer.

"Hello," he said. It was six o'clock.

"What the hell happened to you?" Tucker said. "I've been able to piece bits and pieces together, but I want to know your side. I've been worried sick about you and almost flew home."

Sitting up in bed, a grin spread across his face.

"Hello, cousin, how are you?"

"I'm in damn London, and I'd rather be home at the ranch," he said. "Five more cities and we're done. So tell me what happened, so I can contact law enforcement."

For the next fifteen minutes, Jacob told him what he remembered from the incident.

"You're lucky to be alive," he said. "That particular gang is responsible for three deaths."

A chill went through Jacob. Their intent had been to kill him that night and something spooked them.

"Well, I hear the leader took a trip to hell that night," he said. "Courtesy of my cash."

"I'd rather he was behind bars. How much money was in your wallet?"

"Over a thousand dollars," Jacob said. "I keep most of it hidden in my secret compartments, which I'm sure they found."

Tucker chuckled. "He certainly had one last high."

"Tanner told me my truck was in pieces," he said.

"You should start searching for a new vehicle," he told him. "Yours will never be the same, even if they could find it all. One of my informants told me it was stripped down to the frame. Sold for parts."

Jacob sighed. He'd really liked that truck and hated that it had been treated that way. Now that he could remember everything, the memory of that night left him cold. How in the hell had he survived?

"I'll be emailing you some mug shots I want you to look at. We're going to do our best to get these bastards."

As much as he hated what they had put him through, he didn't know if he wanted to seek revenge on them. After all, he had met Hannah because of them. But the thought of them doing this again was enough to make him agree.

"I don't want them to hurt anyone else," he said. "I lost my memory for a week. If they hadn't been interrupted, I would be dead."

"Who helped you?"

For the next few minutes, they talked about Hannah. How she stopped and picked him up when he was wandering down the road, a lost soul without knowing who he was. Tucker got a laugh out of how she promised to taze him if he tried anything.

"What's her last name?"

"Hannah Christenson," he said. "We've got to keep her out of the news. All I know is that she doesn't want anyone to know she's here. Especially her family."

Tucker was silent for a moment. "What if she's part of the gang?"

"No," Jacob said, knowing that couldn't be true. He'd be devastated to learn she had been a member of those jerks. Besides, she was the heiress from New York that was missing. Or was she?

"Hear me out," Tucker said. "What if her family is the gang and she's trying to escape them."

That couldn't be true. Besides, she'd driven up after he was out of town.

"No," Jacob said. "I don't believe it. She's an artist. She can paint like you wouldn't believe. She's on her way to visit the home of her idol, Georgia O'Keefe."

There was a moment of silence and then Tucker said, "You don't even know that Christenson is her real name."

That was true, but he wouldn't admit it to Tucker. "Why would she lie?"

"She doesn't want to be found," Tucker said.

That was true. She might have lied to him to keep him from telling her family where she was at. In his eyes, the woman was an angel who rescued him, and he didn't believe anything bad about her.

"Look, she's taken care of me for a week. She's fed me and did her best to convince me to see a doctor. You want to find the people who did this to me. But she's a good person. I've slept in the back seat of her old SUV for days. We traveled from campsite to campsite, and I watched as she painted the landscape. Yes, she's a very private person, but she's not a criminal."

There was silence. One thing about his cousin, he took the safety and security of the family very seriously.

"I'm glad you're all right. We were all so worried and when I saw who the police thought attacked you, I feared the worst," he said. "The leader was wanted for armed robbery, drug trafficking, murder, and a whole list of smaller crimes. He was a mean dude."

"I'm just glad I remember who I am and where I'm from. Not knowing who you are is a terrible feeling," he said. "Speaking of, Aunt Rose is insisting I go see the family doctor, so I guess I better get up and get going. She even called him last night at midnight to make an appointment."

When he got home, there had been a message from the doctor telling him to be in his office at eight o'clock this morning.

Five minutes later, he hung up the phone and jumped in the shower.

As he stepped out, the smell of lavender hit him in the face. Why was he smelling that now? There was no lavender in his bathroom. No, he didn't believe in the ghost, and yet last night, she'd been there with the whole family. Or was that just an image projected to make him believe?

How could he deny she existed?

"Jacob, are you decent?"

And what was she doing here now?

"No," he said. "I'm naked and I don't believe in you. You're a prank my cousins pulled on me last night. I've yet to figure out how they're doing this, but you tell them it's not very funny to a man who is recovering from a robbery."

There was an old woman's cackle as he wrapped a towel around himself and then stood in front of the mirror shaving.

The image of an old woman flickered behind him in the mirror.

He cursed and nicked his chin. It had been a while since he'd shaven with a good razor. Hannah had given him one of hers, but he liked his much better.

"Jacob. You're a Burnett, and Burnett men are gentlemen. They don't curse. Clean up your language or I'll wash your mouth out with soap."

"You and what army?"

He turned and stuck his arm through the apparition.

"Oh, that tickles," she said with a laugh.

"Travis, this is not funny," he said. "And, Joshua, if you're behind this, I will tell your daughters how much of a hound dog you were growing up. I'll tell all your secrets that I know of and maybe even make some up."

There was silence.

"Get dressed, Jacob, we need to talk," the old woman said. "I'll be waiting for you in the bedroom. Don't come out in your underwear."

"You're in my space," he told the woman. "How are they projecting you inside my house?"

She faded out of view and he picked up the hair dryer and blew his dark hair dry.

Going into the closet, he took his time getting dressed. Let the supposed ghost wait. Besides, it felt so good to wear something besides that awful shirt and jeans.

He was going to talk to Travis and even Joshua today about how this was not the time for them to be playing pranks on him.

Plus, he wanted to check the rodeo schedule and see when he could ride next. For the moment, he wasn't ready to give up his dream of being a professional bull rider, though damn, that last bull made him question his decision.

Was it the hit from the bull or the whack on the head from the robber that caused him to lose his memory? And no, he never wanted to experience that again.

But being a professional bull rider was his dream just like painting was Hannah's. The thought of her made his chest warm. Could he sneak in and kiss her good morning?

With a sigh, he pulled on his jeans and a starched shirt, he grabbed a new pair of boots and walked into the bedroom, hoping the vision was gone.

She sat in a chair in the corner of the bedroom.

"I'm going to find out where they are transmitting your image from and I'm going to shut this down," he said. "This is not right. After everything I've been through, I don't need them pranking me."

The woman laughed. "I love it when you Burnett men get all stubborn on me. I'm, as you kids say, the real deal. I'm your great-great-great-great-grandmother, Eugenia Burnett. One of the original owners of this ranch. Though at the time only the main house and the barns were on the property. Then we added a home for Tanner and Beth."

"Uh-huh," he said, sitting on the bed and pulling on his boots. Maybe if he ignored her, she would go away. Besides, he knew the family history.

"I'm here because it's time for you to marry," Eugenia said.

"I'm all about the continuation of this family. The more the merrier. You've reached the age and it's time."

"Of course, it is," he said. "Isn't that what you're known for? Our matchmaking grandmother."

He'd been told about her since he was a little kid, but he didn't believe in ghosts and thought the stories were bullshit.

"Yes," she said, grinning. "I've helped all the Burnetts find love. And Hannah is perfect for you."

He did like Hannah, a lot. But she had a dream she was pursuing. And as much as he'd like to go with her to New Mexico, he had his own dreams. Dreams that included riding another bull.

Though kissing Hannah last night had felt so good. So right, and yet, she'd been the one to pull back. He'd held back for a week, not knowing if there was someone else in his life, but not any longer. He planned on kissing her often and deeply.

"Well, good for you," he said. "I'm glad you've helped them, but I'm not quite ready to get married. So if you'll excuse me, I need to leave and get to the doctor."

The woman stood and floated in front of him.

"Hannah is in some kind of trouble and you need to marry and protect her," she said. "You two are perfect for one another."

How was she so certain that Hannah was the right woman for him? And how did his cousins know this since they were the ones programming this image in front of him? They knew nothing about Hannah. None of this made sense.

Since yesterday, he'd realized that Hannah had secrets. Secrets she insisted on hiding.

Sooner or later, he hoped she would tell him, but until

then, he most certainly liked the way she felt in his arms, the smell of her, and her laughter. The woman was serious about pursuing her dreams and he was not going to stop her.

A person's dreams made them happy.

"Do you love her?" the ghost asked.

Speechless, he stared at his grandmother. "That is none of your business."

You couldn't fall in love with someone within a week, could you? Wouldn't it take months? Years? And yet, the thought of her leaving made his chest ache and his stomach clench.

No, he didn't want her to leave. But that didn't mean they were meant to be husband and wife.

"I gotta go," he said, grabbing his hat hanging on a dresser hook and walking toward the door. "I've got to get to the doctor. Tell Travis this shit has got to stop."

If the ghost or whatever it appeared she was spoke to him, was she also speaking to Hannah?

He turned and walked back into the bedroom and stood before the apparition. "Do not disturb Hannah. She needs her rest and please don't tell her that you are going to match us. Leave her be."

Already, she'd resisted and pulled back from his kiss. That might push her over the edge and have her jumping in that old SUV and hauling her trailer and herself out of here. Before she traveled alone again, he wanted to make certain that her car and the trailer didn't need any mechanical work. It was the least he could do for her.

The image laughed at him.

He hoped Joshua and Travis were enjoying this. Payback was a bitch.

Why did he get the feeling that already this image had spoken to Hannah?

Why did it feel like it was too late?

"I'm leaving. Let Hannah sleep."

With that, he turned on his heel and walked out of the bedroom. When he reached the front door, it was so tempting to walk down the hall to see if Hannah was all right.

It would be better if he left her alone too. As much as he was tempted by her, she had a wall of resistance between them. Maybe she wasn't into him like he was her.

But could he leave her alone? And did he want to? Oh no. Even now, walking without her, he was tempted to run back in and pull her out of that bed and kiss her until she was senseless then crawl under the covers with her.

But was that what she wanted?

CHAPTER 14

*H*annah needed to get back on the road and continue her journey. Every day, she was tempted more and more by Jacob. The man was as decent a man as she'd ever met and the smell of him, his touch, even his voice, seemed to resonate deep inside her.

Today, he was checking out her car while she painted the ranch landscape. Already, he'd replaced the brakes and she'd painted the rolling hills with the cattle in the distance. The big oak trees must've been over a hundred years old.

There was a peacefulness about the ranch, even with the guests they were hosting who wanted to be weekend cowboys. She avoided them, fearing that someone would recognize her.

After all, her family often appeared on the society pages, and she didn't want anyone contacting her father and saying they found her. *She's down here in Texas on a ranch.*

This morning, she had planned on packing up and leaving, but Jacob told her to wait one more day. To let him check out her car and she had.

But tomorrow she needed to leave. The more she was around people, the more chances that someone would recognize her. It was time to get back on her journey to finalize her dreams, and yet, the thought of leaving Jacob was almost unbearable.

As much as she wanted him, it could never be, but she didn't want to walk away without him knowing the truth.

Damn her situation. Damn her father for making it impossible for her to live her life the way she wanted.

She gazed out at the panorama, almost finished with the painting she wanted to give to Jacob. This was his home and he loved it here. This would be her farewell gift to him. Hopefully, when he gazed at the painting, he would think of her with fondness. And she would never forget him.

With a sigh, she leaned back from the easel and gazed at him.

"That's beautiful," a woman behind her said. "You're really good."

"Thank you," she said.

The woman had ridden up on horseback behind her and she hadn't even heard her, she'd been so engrossed with getting just the right shade of blue sky and green grass.

"Do you do family portraits?"

"Yes," Hannah said. "But I like to do them outdoors."

"That's what I want," the woman said. "We're here on vacation and it would be perfect. I want that background and us sitting out here."

It would be a simple enough painting and wouldn't take too long. The people would be the hardest to paint. But she was going to leave in the morning.

"How much do you charge?" the lady asked.

Hannah thought of the other portraits she'd done in the past and came up with an extreme amount hoping to discourage the woman so that Hannah didn't have another reason to stay.

"I charge five thousand dollars," she said.

The woman smiled. "Deal. Can you do it tomorrow? We leave on Saturday."

Stunned the woman did not even flinch at the price, she knew that money would get her through the rest of her trip. She could travel on to New Mexico on Saturday and she'd have plenty of money for the journey home.

A grin spread across her face. "Be here at nine a.m. and it will take me a couple hours to paint you."

Tomorrow, she had every intention of leaving, but she could finish this portrait, collect her money, and be on the road the next day.

That would also give Jacob time to finish working on her car. She kept telling him, he didn't have to do that, but he insisted. And it felt good for someone to be worried about her safety.

"I'm so thrilled," the woman said. "I'll have my husband and son here in the morning. Thank you."

The woman trotted off and Hannah smiled.

When she finished the landscape, she took out a blank canvas and quickly painted another one like the one she had created for Jacob. Tomorrow morning, all she would have to do was put the people in the picture and it would be done.

The sun was setting when she heard a golf cart come to where she was painting.

"Hey, you," Jacob said as he parked the cart and walked toward her.

God, the man was so handsome. Her heart fluttered in her chest, and for the thousandth time, she wished her life was different.

"What did the doctor say?" she asked him. "Are you all right?"

A frown crossed his face. "He said for me to stay off bulls for at least two months. One more blow to my head right now could be my last."

The paintbrush floated in her hand when she turned to him. She remembered he'd said he wanted to be a professional bull rider, and she didn't know what to say to him. This was his dream.

"What are you going to do?"

"I don't know," he said. "It's all I ever wanted to do. It was bad enough that I hit my head in the rodeo arena, but when that jerk knocked me in the skull, that's what caused me to lose my memory. The doctor said that's very serious and advised me to be very careful for the next six months. And he advised against ever riding a bull again."

The memory of her family scoffing at her wanting to paint struck her, and as much as she cared for Jacob, she could not tell him to never ride a bull again.

"Can you wear a helmet?"

"Already do," he said.

She put the paintbrush down and stood. Taking his hand in hers, she gazed into his sapphire eyes. "I can't imagine someone telling me I could never paint again. You have to decide what you can live with or without. Can you be happy never being a professional bull rider?"

Jacob looked off and licked his lips. "I don't know. It's something I've got to think about."

Nodding, she told him, "Only you can decide."

Suddenly he pulled her against him. "God, Hannah. You're the only one who understands. Everyone else has told me to stop. But you have a dream. You realize how you have to do what you love."

Her arms came up and wrapped around his neck and it felt like the most natural place to be. In Jacob's arms. Holding him while he dealt with the possible death of his dream. She couldn't even imagine.

"I've placed first in all the local rodeos and was hoping to make it to Vegas just once to ride in the National Finals Rodeo. Just once."

Holding him, she felt his anguish, but she didn't say anything.

Leaning back, he stared into her eyes. "I know you're going to leave soon and I understand. And how I want to go with you. But I've got another rodeo this next weekend and I've got to make some decisions."

His mouth came down, and he covered her lips with his. It was a passionate kiss she shouldn't be enjoying. What she was doing was wrong, and yet, it felt so right, she couldn't give it up.

Leaning into him, she sagged against him, wanting him, needing him, and trying to comfort him the best she could without saying any words. Tomorrow would be the end of this. Tomorrow was her last day here and she would tell him the truth before she left.

They broke apart, their breathing heavy.

"As much as I want you to go with me, it's better that I go alone," she said, becoming much too attached to this man. His gentle nature, his kindness, his protectiveness, and the way he had watched over and cared for her were addicting.

"Will you come back?" he asked.

That was a question she didn't know if she could answer. Would he even want her to come back if he learned the truth about her?

"I don't know. If you want me to, maybe," she said, thinking how hard it would be to leave him a second time.

Staring down at her, he lifted her hat from her head and brushed back her hair from her face. "I realize we haven't known each long, but it's been an intense week."

A grin spread across her face. "Yes, it has."

"And I want you to know I've never felt like this about a woman before. I'm not the Burnett boy who chased after women. Like you, I've been focused on my dreams, not the other sex."

Unable to resist, she reached up and stroked his face with her fingers. "It's one of the things I like so very much about you. A woman knows these kinds of things and…"

She closed her eyes. Not yet, she couldn't tell him yet. They had one more day together. One more and then, he would hate her.

"Take me horseback riding. Show me the place that you love. Let's spend as much time as possible together before I have to leave."

A smile spread across his face. "I can't do horseback riding just yet. The doctor banned me from it for now. But we could pack up a picnic and see the ranch in the golf cart."

"I'd like that very much," she said. "Let me put my paints away and then we can go," she said.

As she packed up her gear, he saw the painting of the ranch. "My God, this is beautiful."

What he didn't know was that he was looking at the painting she was giving him. It was a small piece of herself that she could leave behind.

"If Aunt Rose sees this, she's going to want you to do one for the guest house," he said. "I've never seen anything so beautiful. You captured the essence of the ranch."

Those were the perfect words to hear and her heart soared at his praise. Only her art teachers had praised her before. To hear it coming from Jacob was a wonderful gift.

"Thank you. It's a beautiful place," she said. "You're very lucky."

"I know," he said sadly. "I could never leave this place, but I just wanted to do something on my own. Some small thing that would make me more than just a man from the Burnett Ranch."

She hugged him. "You're Jacob, a wonderful man who doesn't let life get him down, even when it knocks him over the head."

"Yes, but I wanted that rodeo belt buckle," he said. "And the winnings are not too bad either."

Coming apart, her heart ached for him. Could the man give up his dream?

He picked up the painting and put it in the back of the golf cart.

Then he helped her onto the seat and they took off to his house.

"Give me five minutes and I'll be ready to go," she said.

"I'm going down to the kitchen and see if Emily can make

us a picnic basket. We'll take it up to the ridge and watch the sunset there."

It sounded so perfect. Unlike the fancy dinners her father had forced upon her.

"I can't wait," she said. "Anything but hot dogs."

He grinned. "Now, my hot dogs are pretty darn good."

"Yes, they are," she said as she went into the house and he headed toward the building where the kitchen for their guests was.

She hurried into the bedroom, wanting to get out of her painting clothes. Tonight, she wanted to look nice for Jacob.

As she was changing, the smell of lavender filled the room.

"Hannah, dear," she said. "Going somewhere?"

"Jacob and I are having a picnic and watching the sun go down," she said.

"How romantic," the ghost said.

She had to tell the ghost they would never be together.

"Eugenia, I care so much about Jacob, but we can't be a couple."

"Why not, dear? You're perfect for him," she said.

And Jacob was perfect for her. The thought stunned her.

Sinking down on the bed, she put her face in her hands. "I'm falling in love with Jacob."

"That's wonderful, dear. I'm so happy," she said.

"No, you don't understand. I can't marry him. I can't fall in love with him," she said, her heart breaking.

"Whatever is causing you such distress, you need to tell Jacob. Together, the two of you can figure out how to fix this problem," Eugenia said. "Tell him, dear, before you hurt him."

Was this how she wanted to spend tonight? No. As much as it pained her, tonight, she just wanted to enjoy being with him. Tonight was all about the two of them, and then tomorrow, she would tell him the truth and hope that she didn't hurt him as badly as she knew she was going to.

"Not tonight, Eugenia. Not tonight. Tonight I want to enjoy being with Jacob. Tomorrow, I'll tell him."

CHAPTER 15

*J*acob had one more errand before he wanted to spend the evening with Hannah. One more person he wanted to speak with. As he walked into the Burnett headquarters, he went past the receptionist, straight to Travis's office.

He stopped right in front of his cousin's desk, irritated.

"I don't believe in ghosts," he said. "How are you transmitting into my house?"

Travis glanced up from some paperwork and smiled. "We're not. That transmission is straight from the grave."

"That's not possible," he said.

"Oh. Not even your great-great-great-great-grandmother?"

"Hell, no," Jacob said. "Yet, she's in my house. I want her gone."

Travis snickered. "Now you understand why I didn't want my wife's TV ghost show coming to our ranch. Now you understand what we're all talking about when we say grandmother has arrived to find you your mate. Welcome to the club."

Jacob shook his head. It couldn't be true. It just wasn't possible. He didn't want to belong to the club.

"I didn't believe you. I still don't know what to believe, but the smell of lavender permeates my house. She showed up while I was in the shower. I was naked."

He still couldn't believe the old woman had stood in his bathroom with him only wearing a towel. Maybe he should have dropped the cloth to see how fast she disappeared.

Leaning back in his chair, Travis laughed loud enough that Joshua came through the office door.

"What's going on in here?"

"I'll let your brother tell you."

"I have a ghost in my house," he said. "I don't believe in ghosts."

Joshua grinned. "So when is the wedding?"

"What?" Jacob said. "I just got home."

"Brother, once Eugenia sets her sights on you, you might as well surrender and just ask the woman to marry you. Believe me, I know from personal experience. And don't make her angry. She can get mean. When Kayla left me, the woman poured out an entire bottle of my favorite scotch."

Travis shook his head. "Surrender, Jacob. You're next. We've all been through what you're going through and that little lady is very determined. No wonder this family has continued for over one hundred years."

But he wasn't certain that Hannah wanted him. There were walls between them he hadn't been able to breach. Tonight, he had a special picnic planned and he hoped she would let her barriers down and really talk to him about her life.

Something wasn't quite right, and he didn't know what. At least not yet, though the urge to pick her up and carry her into his house and into his bed rode him hard. Now that he knew he was not attached to anyone, he wanted Hannah, and he wanted her to know his feelings.

But, first, he'd come here looking for answers, and instead, all he was receiving were smirks.

"I came to get some practical advice from you about how to get rid of the smell of lavender and an old woman that keeps showing up in my house, and you two are laughing your butts off at me."

The two men chuckled.

"That's because we've been through what you're going through, and while in the end, everything turned out great for us, I wouldn't want to face Eugenia again. She's a tough cookie," Joshua said as he leaned against the wall in Travis's office, his arms crossed.

"Good luck," Travis said. "You might want to start looking at rings now because I'm going to predict that you're married in the next couple of months."

This was not going anywhere.

He glanced at his watch. "I've got to go. I'm taking Hannah up to Lookout Hill."

The two men nodded, a knowing smirk still on their faces.

"Just remember that Eugenia will be waiting for you to return," Travis said.

"And she's very protective of the women she chooses for us," Joshua said. "Believe me, I learned that the hard way as well."

"Go get 'em, tiger," Travis said, laughing.

Shaking his head, Jacob walked out of the office and past the empty receptionist's desk. The woman must have gone home.

Outside, he picked up the basket Emily had prepared for them and then drove up to the house where Hannah sat outside waiting for him.

"Are you ready?"

"Yes," she said, climbing into the golf cart.

Smiling, he took the road they used for the morning rides up to Lookout Hill where he knew they would have a great view of the setting sun.

As soon as they pulled up to the old oak tree that rose from the hillside overlooking the property, they crawled out of the golf cart.

"The ranch is beautiful," she said.

"Thanks, I didn't always live here," he said. "My parents had their own place down the road a ways."

When he thought of his parents, he thought of two people always arguing. They had never been happy, and he never wanted to subject his children to that kind of life. So he was determined that whoever he married would be a good fit. And though his grandmother seemed certain he'd found the right woman, he wasn't. He still had doubts.

When you watched a relationship disintegrate right before your eyes, you weren't certain that it wouldn't happen to you as well. And he had to know and trust whoever he married.

It was the perfect evening. Even the mosquitos were kind and kept their distance as they sat up on the rocky ridge and watched the sun descend.

Emily had fixed them a lovely picnic with cheese, fruit,

and sliced meats they could put on either bread or crackers. And she'd included a bottle of wine which Jacob opened and they shared.

Never had he felt so good as they sat there and watched the sun fall in the sky.

"I'm surprised you didn't bring your camera," he said.

"No, tonight, I'm taking off. Mother Nature will have to put on another show for me another time."

It was nice that she wanted to spend her evening with him and only him. They had pushed aside talking about his health scare and even her leaving. But he had questions he needed answers to.

"Tell me about your family," he said. "Do you have brothers and sisters?"

He wanted to learn more about her. He needed to understand her better if Eugenia thought she was the perfect match for him, he had to be certain. It felt good to know he was falling in love with this woman.

There was a calmness about her that he enjoyed, which was different from his memories of his mother. He liked the way Hannah knew what she wanted, and being with her felt easy and natural. But still, there were so many things about her that he didn't know.

"I have two younger sisters," she said. "My parents have been married for almost thirty years. My mother was a debutante that my father managed to snatch away from twenty other men or so my father says."

A debutante. Sounded like her family was wealthy. Just like his mother's family had been well-to-do, and his father had been a Burnett cowboy working the ranch. When they married, his father had money, but not like his mother's family. They were into the social scene and the Burnetts were just ordinary folks.

"What does your father do for a living?"

A frown drew her brows together. "He owns a hedge fund company. Some years it does very well and other years he promises us we're going to be living on the streets. This year is a living-on-the-streets year."

She gave a little laugh. "He's quite the drama king. Always looking for his next million dollars."

Jacob couldn't imagine telling his children if they were in financial trouble.

"Some years the cattle make us money, and some years, they are just a liability we take care of," he said. "But we always know it's going to get better."

"Exactly," she said. "Dad likes to take us to the edge, glance over, and peer down before he backs away. Maybe that's the reason I got into art, so I didn't have to listen to his numbers philosophy any longer."

Now he wondered if she would tell him why she didn't want her family to know where she was. It just seemed strange that she had no cell phone, nothing. And he worried that someday she would need one when she got into trouble.

"So why don't you want them to know where you are?"

"Because they would make me come home. He likes to threaten that he will cut off my money if I don't do what he says. My trust fund is what I live on while I'm waiting to make money with my art. Someday I hope to be able to walk away from him and his money, but in the meantime, I need it if I want to paint."

Jacob was so glad that when the Burnett children turned twenty-one, they were given their trust fund and it was up to them to make their way with or without the money. No one held it over their head. There were no restrictions on how they could use their inheritance.

And if they blew it, they were not given a second chance.

Right now, he could walk away from the ranch and never have to worry again, but not everyone was as lucky. Not everyone was a billionaire and lived like an ordinary person.

"I'm concerned that you don't have a cell phone. What if you break down? That SUV you're driving is not in the best shape. I've done all the repairs, but frankly, you need to slide a new car in there. Not that junker."

A smile spread across her face as she glanced at him. They were sitting on a bench the family had put up here for this purpose. A place to watch the sun disappear below the horizon.

"Thank you for doing that. But no, a cell phone can be tracked. Just let me have this trip to New Mexico and then I will do what he requires."

Glancing away from him, she sighed and shook her head.

That sounded strange.

"What does he require?"

She turned to him. "Tonight is about us enjoying one another. Let's not talk about my family and how screwed up that situation is. Your family seems normal, and I love the land where you live. It's beautiful. Can we please enjoy tonight and each other? Tomorrow, I have to leave after I paint the Gregg family."

She was slamming the walls back into place and ending the questions. Why? What was so bad that her father wanted her to do? What did he require?

"Does he want you to give up your dreams?"

A chuckle came from her. "He's tried to get me to give up painting since I was twelve. At this point, I would paint with my toes if I had to just to keep him from winning."

With a sigh, she gazed at the sky. "Look at that sunset. The streaks of orange and the different shades. It's so hard to paint the canvas of God. My strokes will never be that beautiful."

Her head tilted and she frowned.

"You've never told me about your parents. Where are they? Do they live here on the ranch?"

Jacob stared as the sky turned a shade of blue as night approached. She deserved to know about his past just as much as he wanted to know about hers.

"My mother died of breast cancer. By the time she got sick, she'd destroyed our family. You see, she was a drunk who liked to party. She cheated on my dad who was the rock of our family. He didn't deserve to be treated that way," he said, sighing. "Even though they were divorced, her death just about killed my father. Not long after she was gone, he died. They had not been happy for years. It's one of the reasons I hate hospitals. They remind me of her death."

"Oh my," she said. "I'm so sorry."

"It's why trust is so important to me," he said softly. "My mother cheated on my father, and I want nothing to do with anyone who isn't honest. I'm not going to live the life my parents led. I'm not going to subject my children to the constant arguing and bickering that I witnessed between my parents."

For just a second, she glanced away and tensed.

"Honesty and trust are the framework of a good relationship. I won't accept anything less," he said.

"How old were you?"

"I was twelve," he said. "My brother Joshua was fourteen at the time. He grew up to be like my mother – a different woman all the time, never committing to anyone. Until he learned he was a father. Then the nanny helped him become the man he is today. And I'm so happy for him. He's a good man.

"Justin is still dealing with a sharp tongue. He pretty much hates women because of our mother. He's distrustful of people and he's cranky. He was eight when Mother died."

"That's not good," she said.

No, it wasn't. In fact, Justin spent a lot of time alone. He didn't want to be around people. He didn't need them. What he really needed was the love of a woman.

"When and if I marry, the woman I choose must be honest with me. My children will never be put through the hell that my brothers and I went through. Not going to happen."

Or at least, he would do everything humanly possible to keep it from happening again.

"You're a good man, Jacob," she said. "Any woman would be lucky to have you."

The sun sank beneath the horizon and he glanced at her.

Why did it feel like she was still keeping secrets from him? Why did it feel like she'd not been completely honest with him? Was he just being paranoid?

And did she not realize he was falling so hard for her? But he had to know the truth about her before he could tell her he loved her.

Damn, Eugenia was right. You could fall in love with someone in a week and he'd never intended to. But life slammed them into each other's paths and now he wanted her so badly.

"Come on, it's time we headed back," he said. "It's getting dark and we don't want to step on a rattler."

With a sigh, she stood. "Thanks for tonight. I loved everything about it."

Pulling her up to him, his lips covered hers and he told her with his mouth what his heart was feeling. If only she would tell him what she was hiding from him. If only she would be honest.

He would fight her battles for her. He would tell her father to jump off a high cliff. That he loved his daughter and wanted to protect her. Right now, Jacob would do anything to help Hannah. Anything.

Placing her hands between them, she pushed away from him.

"I can't," she said. "Oh, how I want to, but I can't."

"Why not?"

"Please, don't ruin tonight. I want to remember this time with you."

Stepping back, she ran and jumped into the golf cart, leaving him standing on the edge of the hill.

"Take me back to the house," she said.

Reluctantly, Jacob walked to the golf cart.

"Sooner or later, you're going to have to tell me," he said.

With a deep sigh, she wiped tears from her eyes. "Not tonight."

CHAPTER 16

J acob had tossed and turned all night. This
morning, he was out of the house, determined to
stay busy.

Hannah had said she was leaving today after she painted
the Gregg family. If only he could convince her to stay. If only
he could promise her that he would take her to Abiquiu.

This morning, he had chores that needed to be done, and
then he was going to confront Hannah one more time. Try to
find out what was bothering her and why she couldn't
kiss him.

Last night, she'd pushed him away, and he knew from
experience that she enjoyed his kiss. She reacted to the feel of
his lips on hers. So why didn't she want him kissing her? Why
did she keep throwing up blocks between them?

Two hours later, he had helped saddle the horses for their
guests to be taken out on a ride, which Travis or Tanner
always led.

The eggs were gathered. After the rattlesnake in the hen

house, they no longer allowed their guest to gather the eggs. The pigs were fed and he'd had some breakfast that Emily cooked.

Now he needed to find Hannah and demand some answers.

When he walked back from the community center to his home, he saw her sitting outside painting the family that had requested their portrait done with the ranch in the background.

Coming up behind her, he watched her paint the Gregg family. The man and son looked like they were ready to bolt any second.

"If you don't hurry, we're going to miss the trail ride," the man said.

"Honey, she's getting close. Just think, we'll have our family portrait here on the ranch."

The man frowned and Jacob could tell the man didn't really care about the picture. Obviously, this was the woman's idea. Their son stood there, rolling his eyes and popping his gum, appearing bored.

"What time does the trail ride leave?"

"The horses are saddled and waiting for everyone to come down from breakfast," Jacob told him.

With a sigh, the man stood there a little longer.

"I'm giving you ten minutes and then I'm done," the man said. "We've been doing this for nearly an hour."

Finally, Hannah glanced at the family. "I've got enough done that you can go enjoy your day. I'll have this finished soon and I'll have it delivered to your room."

"Thank you," the woman said relieved.

The man shook his head. "Come on, let's go before they leave us."

Grabbing his wife's hand, he pulled her down the road toward the stables.

He watched with fascination as Hannah put the final finishing strokes on the painting. She'd captured the softness of the woman and the stern expression of the man and the bored look on the kid's face. In time, they would look back on this painting and think how they had been so different then.

"The ladies invited me to lunch today," she said, grinning. "They wanted to meet the woman that had saved Jacob."

Hope filled his heart. The women were including her in their weekly lunches. Not long after they all started having babies, the wives decided to meet once a week to talk about their children and discuss their men. The Burnett men who they adored.

"Are you going?"

"Oh, yes," she said, smiling.

"Don't believe everything you hear about me," he told her.

A frown flitted across her face and then she sighed. "Of course." She bit her lip. "I decided to delay leaving today. I'll pull out in the morning."

His heart tightened and he sighed. "I understand. I wish I could go with you, but I need to stay here and do my share."

There was a big group coming in next week and Aunt Rose had said all hands on deck, which meant no one was going to be missing. Everyone would need to help with their guests. Including Jacob.

With her leaving, he couldn't wait any longer. Last night, his feelings had bothered him all night. He had to tell her how she made him feel.

"Hannah, I know you have to leave. I know we've only known each other for a little more than a week, but during that time, my heart was like a blank canvas. You came into my life and you've thrown splashes of color I've never considered before on my heart.

"In just one week, I've gotten to know you. Your quirkiness. Your laugh. Your determination to get to where you want to go. When you picked me up that night, I was hurting so badly, and frankly, I just wanted to die. And yet you took me in, you comforted me, you did your best to heal me. There's so much I don't know about you, but I'm falling in love with you."

A gasp escaped her and he pulled her up from her chair and took her into his arms. "Wait and let me go with you to Abiquiu. Stay here with me and let's get to know each other better."

"Oh, Jacob," she gasped against his chest. "You and I, we can't."

"Why not?" he asked, his voice frustrated. "Don't you like me?"

She leaned her head down on his chest. "I like you way more than I should."

"Then what is holding you back? Tell me so I can fix the problem," he said.

It was so frustrating that she hadn't told him what kept her from committing to him. She felt something for him or she would have pulled back even more. But there was a barrier between them that he just couldn't get through.

Leaning back, she jerked in his arms, her body going tense. Suddenly she stepped away from him, shaking her head.

"No. No. No. Daddy?"

Whirling around, Jacob saw a well-dressed man, flanked by Travis and Joshua, walking toward them. A large black limo sat in the driveway to the main house. The man glared at him as he stalked like a drill sergeant.

Was this man Hannah's father?

"No," Hannah whispered. "Please, no."

CHAPTER 17

*H*annah felt like someone had knocked the breath from her body. With a loud gasp, she watched as her father strode toward her like a vision from hell. He was here at the Burnett Ranch and he was madder than a bee who'd lost his hive.

How had he found her?

She was so screwed. There would be no trip to New Mexico to visit her favorite painter's home. All her plans were ruined. She'd been found.

Even worse, what would he do to Jacob?

"This is not how it looks," she said when he walked up to her and Jacob, his eyes flashing with anger. Thank goodness he wasn't a fighter, but he was still a mean son of a bitch.

A snarky smile spread across his face and she knew it was his mad facial expression. The one he used when he was so angry that he would retaliate for months and make her life a living hell.

As a child, she had learned to run when she saw that mean snarl. Thank goodness, he never touched her, but he could be

SYLVIA MCDANIEL

mean and ruthless just the same. Sometimes a sharp tongue was just as much of a weapon as a fist.

The entire Burnett family began to gather outside, closing in. Her humiliation would be complete. Here in front of these wonderful people, he would make her out to be nothing.

"Have you enjoyed making your mother sick with worry? With me spending thousands of dollars to find you? Have you enjoyed your bohemian vacation? Because it's over."

Yes, and there would be hell to pay. She'd almost made it to New Mexico. She'd almost gotten to experience her dream. But now everything would fall apart. Everything.

The nights in her little camper, her time with Jacob when they were out on the road, all of that would now be worthless. Just memories to keep her warm when everything was so cold.

"Imagine my surprise when the private investigators I had on the case came across this?"

He held up the nude drawing of Jacob and shoved it toward her.

A giggle went up in the crowd.

"Is that Jacob, in the buff?" Joshua asked.

"I'd pay a thousand bucks for that right now," Travis said, snickering.

Aunt Rose put an elbow in Travis's ribs. The entire family was here watching her disgrace. And her father had only just begun.

"How did you know it was mine?"

"Because you signed your name at the bottom," he said. "You can't read the writing of the last name, but when they showed me what they had found, I knew it was your piece of trash."

Why in the hell had she sold those drawings? Why? They had led him to her. Once they learned the name of the cowboy, then they found her. Could she defy him?

"I'm not going home with you," she said.

"Oh, yes, you are," he said with a determined smile that sent a chill down her spine. "You agreed to the deal. Now it's time you did your part. I'll get my security guards if I have to."

Not really. She had never wanted to be part of his wheeling and dealing. Never. He was the one who insisted she agree to what he needed. He was the one who made her feel like she had no choice. He was the one who would sell her soul if it kept him rich.

"I still have a month. I'm going to Abiquiu," she said, her voice seething.

"No, you're not. You're going home with me now," her father said. "You're done tramping around."

He glanced at Jacob, his lip curled up in a growl.

Jacob stepped in front of her. "Sir, she's come so far from Florida. Let her continue on to her dream."

Tears welled in her eyes. Jacob was fighting for her and then she saw the wicked gleam in her father's eyes and knew what he was going to do.

A pain unlike anything she'd ever felt squeezed her chest and she wanted to scream at him to stop. To shut up. That it wasn't true, but sadly it was. And her father would enjoy plunging the knife into her heart and destroying her.

"Young man, I'm sure my daughter has tricked you into helping her, but here's a little tidbit I'm not quite sure you know. She's not from Florida and she's engaged to be married."

A gasp came from the Burnetts gathered in the yard.

Turning to Jacob, she tried to grab his hand and he stepped back.

"You're engaged?"

"Not because I want to be," she said, tears clogging her throat. "I don't want this wedding. Truly, I don't. I was going to tell you tonight."

"Then why are you marrying him? Do you love him?"

"No," she cried, realizing she wanted to tell Jacob the truth, but her father would be even madder if she said the words out loud. "I have no choice."

"Everyone has a choice," Jacob said. He was furious. "Trust is sacred. I may not have known who I was, but you knew who you were and that you were engaged to be married."

It was true, but she had not expected to fall in love with Jacob. In fact, she'd done her best to avoid the feelings he created inside her heart. If she didn't love him, she would have left yesterday. But she didn't want to say good-bye.

"I didn't expect to get to know you. To enjoy being with you and all the fun we had. I didn't know who you were, but I knew you were a good man. A man any woman would be proud to call hers."

Her father, seeing how upset Jacob was, twisted the knife in further. Everything she wanted was slipping away right in front of her eyes. All her dreams.

"Maxwell is the perfect husband for Hannah. Since your disappearance, he's been very understanding, and I'm shocked he's still willing to marry you. His family is a fine, upstanding New York City family that is wealthy. You and he will be perfect for one another."

But she didn't want to marry Maxwell. With a staggering

blow, she realized her heart belonged to Jacob. The man who even now stared at her like she was evil.

"I didn't expect to fall in love with you," she said.

Another gasp came from the crowd.

"This trip was my last chance to be free before I was forced to marry someone I don't love. I never thought I'd meet a man who accepts me for who I am, appreciates me, and loves my work. No one has ever loved my art before."

Jacob's sapphire eyes flashed with rage and she knew she had hurt him.

"It's a little late to be realizing that," he said in a mocking tone. "You're not from Florida? What about you is true? Was everything a lie?"

From his expression, she could see she had lost him. He wanted someone truthful and honest, and she'd been neither.

"Jacob," she cried, trying to appeal to him. "No, I was hiding, trying not to be found."

"Well, that didn't work out very well," Jacob said, his arms firmly crossed over his chest.

He hated her. She had betrayed him by not being honest with him, and now he would never forgive her.

Glancing at her father, she hated the evil smile on his face. The gleam of satisfaction that he'd destroyed her life.

The smell of lavender filled the air and she wanted to groan. Not Eugenia. Not now.

"Get your things, we're leaving," her father said. "The company jet is waiting for us at DFW."

Just then a big blob of bird poo landed on his shoe.

With disgust, he glanced up at the sky.

"Damn bird," he said. "Get your things. Let's go."

Turning toward Jacob, she pleaded with her eyes. "I'm

sorry. You are the best thing that ever happened to me. I never intended to fall in love with you. Please remember the good times we had together."

He didn't respond, but simply stared at her.

She turned back to her father. "What about my paintings."

A smile spread across his face and he did the most hurtful thing to her. "Leave them. You're not bringing them home. They should be destroyed."

All those paintings she'd created. All the ones along the road to the different parks. Pieces of her life. All were for her plans to do a show when she returned to New York. And he didn't want her to bring them.

To him, they were nothing but trash, but to her, they were the results of a trip filled with love.

Everything was ruined. Despair unlike anything she'd ever felt before overcame her. It was over.

Glancing around at the gathered crowd, she couldn't stop the tears sliding down her cheeks.

"What about my trailer and the car?"

"Farmer Brown here can sell them. He probably needs the cash," her father said with a dismissive wave of his hand. Another plop of bird poo landed on his suit coat.

He cursed. "In the limo, now. Leave it all."

Glancing back at Jacob, she felt the hate radiating from him.

"I'm sorry," she said, her knees knocking, her chest aching from her shattered heart. Slowly, she turned and walked away, knowing she would have to listen to her father berate her all the way home.

She would be required to marry Maxwell.

As she passed Aunt Rose, she blew her a kiss and said thank you.

The older woman nodded, her eyes sad.

A big blob of bird poo landed on her father's head and he cursed again and glanced up at the sky. There was nothing.

"I hate the country. Why am I the only one some bird is pooping on," he cried.

And then the smell of lavender surrounded her as a tear rolled down her cheek and she knew why. It wasn't a bird. It was Eugenia letting her feelings be known about her father.

How she got a bird to poop on her father, she didn't know, but in some small way, she was grateful. If she hadn't been so sad, she would have laughed.

"Thanks, Eugenia," she whispered.

The wind blew and the smell of lavender enveloped her like a hug.

Climbing into the limo, she glanced back at Jacob one last time, her heart smashed.

He stood there, resolute. His arms were crossed and he glared at the limo like he wanted to break it into pieces. Oh, if only he would rescue her, she would never leave him. But that wasn't possible; she had a duty to her family.

Reluctantly, she crawled in. Her adventure was over. Her paintings made her heart ache.

Her father got in the car and slammed the door shut.

"Let's go," he told the driver. "Get me out of the backwoods."

The limo driver put the car in drive and she stared out the back window, wanting one last look at the man she loved.

They pulled through the big iron gates of the Burnett Ranch and she sighed.

"You should have been nicer," she said softly.

"Why? They're just a bunch of cowboy hillbillies. I don't need that," he said.

The man was stupid.

"They're one of the wealthiest families in Texas. They have money in oil and cattle."

Glancing at her, he gave a little laugh.

"Sure they do," he said.

"Your loss," she said, thinking if only he would listen to her, but the man didn't believe anything his wife or daughters said.

"I don't believe you," he said, leaning back against the seat.

"You never do," she replied.

Hugging the door of the limo, she tried to sit as far away as possible from her father. All she wanted was to curl into a ball and cry. All those paintings, gone. But even worse was the loss of Jacob. Now he hated her and she understood why. In fact, he had every right to be angry with her. She should have told him sooner.

When was she going to grow a spine and tell her family to take a hike? When was she going to tell them to never bother her again? Yet, how could she not marry Maxwell when her father told her they would be destitute without Maxwell's family money?

She had to marry him in order to save the family business. Ironic how she didn't even like the family business. But she did care about her sisters and her mother.

For them, she would marry Maxwell and save the family from being homeless, from being run out of New York. But never would she marry for her father. Never.

With a sigh, she leaned her head against the window.

"You are the worst daughter ever. Do you know how much money I spent trying to find you?"

The man began his talk that would not end until they reached New York and she managed to escape to her room.

She was an adult. Why did she feel this need to rescue her family when they didn't even love her? Her sisters loved her, and for them, she would do what had to be done. But her father only wanted to save his ass, and he would do whatever was necessary to save his reputation. Even sell his daughter to the highest wedding bidder.

CHAPTER 18

*J*acob watched as the black limo drove out through the gates of the Burnett Ranch with Hannah inside. It was all he could do not to go running after the car, screaming for it to stop.

He loved her and watching her leave was killing him.

But she was engaged to be married and she'd never said anything about how she was unavailable.

For him, an engagement was almost like being married. You were committed to one another. You were making plans for a life together. All that was left was the ceremony where you said vows in front of a preacher, family, and God.

He wanted to be the man who slipped a ring on her finger and vowed to love her and protect her until death parted them. But someone else was going to do that, not him.

Someone she had agreed to marry.

There should never be another man at this stage, and Jacob was the other man. It had been his pledge to never be that. Just like his mother had cheated on his father, Hannah was cheating on Maxwell and that left him furious.

As the limo disappeared, he stood there stunned, his heart shattered, his soul ripped from his chest.

Joshua came up to him. "I'm sorry."

The whole family surrounded him and patted him on the back and hugged him. Except Aunt Rose.

Suddenly people parted ways and she marched toward him, leaning on her cane, to stand before him. Her eyes flashed and he noted she was frustrated.

"Something isn't right," she said. "Why did she keep saying she had to marry this man? She said she doesn't want this wedding and she had no choice. She made this trip before she was forced to marry someone she doesn't love. Why?"

What did she want him to say? Hannah was old enough. She had a choice in who she married. And she certainly hadn't told him about her engagement and upcoming marriage.

"This is not the dark ages. She doesn't have to marry someone she doesn't want to. She could stop this wedding."

His aunt's eyes grew large, her brows raising as she made a harrumph sound.

"No, young man, you don't understand. Sometimes a woman is forced to do something she doesn't want to for reasons you don't know. If you love her, you better find out those reasons and stop that wedding."

Shaking his head, he stared at his aunt, knowing she could be a tiger in sheep's clothing.

"Aunt Rose, you know my background. Trust is the foundation of a good relationship and she lied to me. How could I ever trust her again?"

"She lied to protect herself. Hannah is not your mother, and you need to get your head out of your ass and see she was in survival mode. Don't let love get away from you because of your pride. You'll regret it for the rest of your life. You're a smart man, Jacob, don't act like a fool."

With that she turned and limped away, leaning heavily on her cane.

Was he wrong to want the truth? To have a partner he could trust? No, he wasn't. Maybe things would look different in a day or two, but right now, he felt like he'd been lied to. Nothing about Hannah was real.

Not even her name.

Travis shook his head. "Her father was an ass. Did you hear what he said about us? He called you Farmer Brown."

"She mentioned him before and said her family could be trying. I'd say he definitely fulfilled what she said about him."

No wonder, she'd escaped if that was the man she had to deal with. But could he make her marry someone she didn't love?

The family was beginning to disperse and he just wanted to get on his horse and go riding, but the doctor had warned him to stay off his horse to avoid being jolted around.

He needed a place to think. A place to get away and lick his wounds and look at what had happened from all sides. A place to compare his mother and Hannah. Were they the same or was there reason to believe she had a good reason for agreeing to marry this Maxwell?

The ATV was too bouncy. The golf cart was his only mode of transportation until the doctor released him. Even his truck was gone and he would need to buy another one. He'd never felt so trapped as he did right now.

"Are you all right?" Joshua asked.

"Yes and no," he said. "I was telling her I loved her when

her father appeared. The man's timing couldn't have been any worse."

Justin came up and clapped him on the back. "It's better not to get involved with women. You're better off without her. Every time I look at a woman, I remember Mom. No, thank you."

The other men groaned. "Your day is coming. Just wait until Eugenia enters your house. You're going to be so screwed. Get ready, she's not going away until she's certain this family will continue."

"You guys must be on crack. I don't believe in ghosts or love or any of this nonsense," Justin said. "Now, I have work to do. Call me if you want to go get a beer."

The man walked off and they all looked at each other and laughed.

Tanner shook his head. "He is going to get gobsmacked by Eugenia."

Travis laughed. "I can't wait to see love grab him around the throat and throttle him."

With a sigh, Jacob watched his little brother walk off. "He's got a lot to learn."

In some ways, he felt sorry for his younger sibling. He'd been hurt the most by their parents' deaths. Looking back, it was probably for the best, but he still missed his father. Even now, he would've loved to speak to his father about how he'd fallen in love with a woman who was engaged.

Shaking his head, he sighed. He needed space. As much as he loved his family, sometimes a man needed to be alone.

"Now, if you'll excuse me. I'm going to take the golf cart up to Lookout Hill and spend some time up there thinking."

The men all nodded and walked away.

What a day. One that he'd hoped would be filled with happiness had turned to sorrow. Deep sorrow and he'd never felt so betrayed.

Could Aunt Rose be right? Could Hannah be forced to marry this man? How? That just didn't make any sense to him. It wasn't like this was the olden days. Women made their own choices and decisions all the time.

Climbing into the golf cart, he headed toward the cliff where he wanted to sit and ruminate. What could he have done differently? Were there signs he missed?

Tonight, he had hoped they would spend the evening making love, but now he understood why she kept resisting his kisses and his attention despite their attraction to one another.

What she'd done was cheating as far as he was concerned.

But why would she marry a man she didn't love? She'd said she loved *him*.

When he reached the hill, the memories of them came flooding back. The way they had shared the sunset last night, sitting here kissing, talking, and enjoying one another's company.

The time together had been peaceful. But she'd known that eventually she would have to tell him the truth. She even hinted that she didn't want to talk about it last night, but just enjoy their time together.

The memory of her sitting and painting hit him in the chest and he realized how it must have killed her to leave her precious paintings behind. Those were her dreams. Just like winning the bull riding competition at the national rodeo was his. Her father had forced her to leave them behind.

What a dick. The man was wealthy enough he could have

made arrangements for them to be shipped, but he'd just whisked her away and made her leave everything behind.

How could her father force her to marry a man she didn't love? In the olden days, he could understand, but not in this day and age.

Maybe he should pack them up and ship them to him. But he didn't know where to send them.

Sitting on the bench, he remembered how she felt in his arms, and finally, tears leaked down his cheeks. The last week of his life had been so damn turbulent and exciting. She'd been so good to him when he couldn't remember his name.

Losing Hannah was like losing a piece of himself. Worse than losing his memory.

By now, she was probably on a plane headed back to New York. It then hit him. He didn't even know her real last name. He had no way of finding her even if he wanted to.

With a sigh, he rose from the bench.

Like a slam to the chest, his emotions overwhelmed him. She was a cheater. It didn't matter that he didn't know her last name. Whatever hope he'd had for their future was over.

They were through. Realizing he didn't know the real her was the final straw. It was over and those paintings would remain locked in her camper. Only, he didn't know what to do with that horrible SUV and trailer.

With his heart breaking, he got back in the golf cart and started down the hill on his way home.

Tonight, he wanted to be left alone.

When he walked into the house, he stopped and stared at the painting she had placed above his fireplace.

It was the one of the ranch like she'd done for the family. Only this one was for him. It was breathtaking and beautiful and it made his heart ache even more. How could he look at that painting every day without thinking of her? Without missing her?

As he walked toward the fireplace, he saw the note.

When he opened the envelope, tears welled in his eyes.

This one is for you. I'm so glad I picked you up on that lonely stretch of highway late that night. I'm leaving in the morning to finish my journey, please come with me. Keep me company. Love, Hannah.

She said she had planned on telling him about her engagement today. But she asked him to go with her. Did an engagement not mean anything to her?

He wiped the tears from his eyes.

The smell of lavender filled the air.

"She loved you."

Shaking his head, he didn't want to talk to his grandmother now.

"Go away, Eugenia," he said.

"It's only over if you let it be. Sometimes women are forced to do things they don't want to do. I don't know for certain that's the problem, but she obviously doesn't love this man she's going to marry. Go talk to her. Find out why she's doing this."

"Why didn't she tell me before now?" he said out loud. "Maybe we could have figured out a way to stop the wedding."

"It's not too late," Eugenia said.

"Yes, it is," he said. "I don't even know her real name."

"Pick up that thing you guys talk to each other on. Get in touch with Tucker," she said.

Jacob thought about it for a moment. Why? Why would he

want to find the woman he was falling in love with that was not the honest person he thought she was?

He walked over to the liquor cabinet and grabbed the bottle of scotch and a glass. Alcohol always reminded him of his mother and he didn't like to partake too much, but today had been one hell of a day.

The last week had been overwhelming. He deserved a drink.

Sinking down in the chair across from the fireplace, he gazed at the painting. Damn, he wanted to take it down, but it was just too gorgeous. The woman could paint.

And she'd painted the place he loved. There was love in her paint strokes. Glancing in the picture's corner, he saw her last name, but he wasn't going to get up and read it. She'd made her decision and he'd made his.

It was over.

He poured himself a glass and stared at the landscape. As a child, he'd played and rode his horse where she painted. This was his land, his family's land, and this was where he belonged.

The only thing missing was her.

Downing the glass, he poured himself another. Memories from the week they traveled together rushed over him. The day he posed naked for her. How he'd felt so embarrassed and yet every one of those drawings sold.

And she'd been discreet with him, looking away at the right moments. If he had known he was available, he would have dropped his hat and strode toward her, but something held him back.

"Are you just going to sit there and get drunk? Why aren't you fighting for this woman?"

"Maxwell is the one who has to fight for her," he said. "She's engaged to him."

And he hated the man even though he'd never met him.

"But she loves you," Eugenia said.

"Maybe so, but I'm not the one marrying someone else."

Tossing back another drink, tonight, he was going to drown his sorrows.

CHAPTER 19

A month later, Hannah stood in front of the multiple mirrors, letting the seamstress do the final dress fitting. She hated this dress. She hated this wedding. She even hated the people here with her. Right now, she hated everything, and she'd made certain that everyone around her knew her feelings.

For the last month, she'd been a terror to be around and even Maxwell had avoided her and that was all right. He was only marrying her for her father's company.

"Hannah," her sister said, gazing at her.

"What do you want?" she said. The wedding was in two days, and with every passing hour, she felt strung tighter than a violin. She was one pluck away from losing her mind.

Every day, she cried when she remembered the way Jacob had stared at her when she left. He hated her and had every reason to feel that way.

Her sister shook her head. "You get worse every day. Why are you doing this?"

A hysterical laugh escaped from her. "What? You don't

believe that I'm madly in love with Maxwell? That he's the man of my dreams?"

As much as she didn't want to marry, she also didn't want her sisters to feel bad that she was doing this for them.

The lady finished with the final alterations. "It's ready, Miss Hannah."

"Thank you," she said, thinking she'd like to grab the scissors from her hands and rip the dress to shreds. Her mother sat in the corner, sipping champagne, and gazing at her phone.

She was her watchdog today. Her father had not let her go anywhere alone. One of her parents had to be with her at all times until she was duly barnacled to her husband-to-be.

The woman motioned for her sister Julie to step up onto the platform where she would check the alterations of her dress.

Hannah went to where the glasses and the champagne were sitting on a tray and poured herself a drink.

"Not in your gown," her mother said, looking up and giving her a stern look. "Take it off before you have anything to drink."

She turned to face her. "Oh, are you afraid I'll spill champagne on my dress? Oh, that would be horrible, wouldn't it? We'd have to call off the wedding."

Her mother stood and removed the glass flute from her hands. "Go change."

Hannah lifted the silk skirt and went into the dressing room. A woman appeared and helped her out of the dress. If only she could escape. But then who would help her sisters and her mother, though the woman didn't seem to care much that she was about to face financial ruin?

Pulling on her clothes, she asked the woman who was hanging up her gown, "Is there a back exit somewhere?"

The woman frowned at her.

"Sorry, it's just everything is getting to me and I'd like to go home," she said.

The woman nodded. "It's down the hall."

"Thank you," she said, hoping she'd have a chance to sneak away.

When she stepped out of the dressing room, her sister Julie was finished. She frowned at her as Hannah hurried to the champagne and picked up her full flute.

"Cheers, Mother," she said. "To the wedding of the year. And a lifetime of being miserable."

With a sigh, her mother shook her head as she watched Hannah tilt the glass up and swallow the entire contents. When she was finished, she gave a loud burp, just because she knew her mother would disapprove.

"Hannah, stop acting like a child," she said.

Oh, already she could feel the resentment inside her exploding and she feared how she would act at the rehearsal dinner. Already, she could see the look of disapproval in Maxwell's eyes, but then again, he was getting a hefty promotion from marrying her. After all, she was the boss's daughter.

His money would keep the business afloat and he would be the chief financial officer married to the girl who sacrificed everything for her family. They would buy an apartment in the city and she would stay home and raise their two-point-five children while he worked with her father.

Her sisters and her mother could continue to live the extravagant lifestyle they were accustomed to and she would be depressed.

Setting the glass down, she asked the woman checking her sister's dress, "Where is the ladies' room?"

"Down the hall," the woman said.

Great, it was near the exit door.

"I'll be back," she said.

Walking toward the ladies' room, she glanced over her shoulder and her mother was watching her. Opening the door, she went inside and did her business.

When she stepped out, her mother was gone.

Quickly, she found the exit and walked outside. As soon as the light from the sun hit her face, she lifted her head.

"Where do you think you're going?" her mother asked.

Damn, double damn.

"I was getting a breath of fresh air," she said, knowing she'd been caught. All she wanted to do was try to call Jacob. To tell him how much she missed him. To hear the sound of his voice one last time.

"Good," her mother said. "Now we can go back in and finish with your sisters' dresses. Then I'll take us all to lunch to celebrate."

A fake smile appeared on her face. "Oh, great, we can celebrate me being sold into slavery."

Her mother frowned. "Quit being so dramatic, dear. Your father has your best interest at heart."

"By forcing me to marry someone I don't love so you and my sisters are well taken care of and his business will survive?"

A funny expression crossed her mother's face.

"Come inside," her mother said, holding the door. "Maxwell is the perfect husband for you."

"According to whom? He's certainly not who I would have chosen," she said. "I don't love him."

"No, you would have chosen a dirty cowboy on a ranch in Nowheresville. You would have been broke."

But that wasn't true. She'd told her father and her mother that the Burnetts were wealthy, but they didn't care. They had their sights set on Maxwell's family money.

With a sigh, she walked back inside to where her youngest sister Sterling was now up on the platform as they checked the dress's hem.

Hannah walked over to the tray and poured herself another glass. She consumed two more glasses of champagne. Anything to make her feel like she could enjoy herself.

When they finished, her sister Julie came over to her. Their mother was paying for the final alterations and arranging for the dresses to be delivered to the house.

"If you don't want to do this, why are you marrying Maxwell?"

If she told her sisters, they would insist that she call off the wedding, not that she thought that would happen. Her father would probably carry her down the aisle in chains if he thought it would do the trick.

What could she tell them?

"The merger of the two families will bring us more money and prosperity," she said using a line from her father.

Her sister frowned. "Why do we need the Thomson's money?"

Julie was too smart for her own good.

"I don't know, ask Father," she said, feeling the effects of the champagne and wanting to go home, go to her room, lie in bed, and stare at the four walls of her prison cell.

"Why aren't you painting?" Julie asked. "You always paint. Ever since you were a little girl, you've painted. In the last month, you haven't even sketched."

Tears brewed in her eyes. Painting had always been her therapy. But her supplies were in her trailer and she had no idea where it was. And all her paintings were inside the trailer.

"I'm over it," she said, missing the feel of paint on her fingers, the brush in her hand, the smell, the design, and the flow as she put the brush to the canvas.

A frown appeared on her sister's face. "What happened while you were gone? You've never told us why you ran away. For weeks, I've avoided asking you because I feared what might have happened to you. This wedding is not what you want and yet you haven't called it off."

Rage exploded inside her, and it wasn't at her sister, but the situation she found herself in. The alcohol had loosened her tongue.

"I ran away to go to New Mexico to visit the home of my favorite painter. To paint where Georgia O'Keefe painted. On the way there, I met a man and fell in love with him. Only problem is that I painted him and sold the drawings. Father found me and brought me home. All my paintings I'd done from here to Texas he made me leave behind."

Her mother walked up and she turned her back to her, her body shaking.

"What's going on here?"

"Oh, Hannah is having pre-wedding jitters," her sister said. "Come on, Mother. You promised us lunch."

Quickly, Hannah wiped her tears away. She turned to face her mother a smile on her face. "Yes, let's go have lunch.

Because I can guarantee that once I'm married and no longer have a watchdog, you won't be seeing me."

Sighing, her mother took Julie by the arm. "I'll be so glad when this wedding is over. Hannah, let's go."

"Of course, Mother dear," she said. "Wouldn't want to be left behind and miss the celebratory lunch. Will Father and Maxwell be there?"

"Yes," her mother said. "Now let's go. The limo is waiting for us outside. When we get to the car, you need to fix your makeup and put on a happy smile. You're the bride, darling, and you're supposed to be happy."

"Well, I'm fucking not," she said.

"Hannah," her mother said, "watch your language."

The lunch was tense and Hannah sat buzzed on champagne and doing her best to smile when all she wanted to do was cry. Finally, it broke up and she went home with her mother and sisters.

Much later that evening, Julie came to her room. Lying in bed, Hannah gazed around the space. Soon, she would no longer live here. Soon, her life would be over and she would have to adjust to her new life.

Her sister plopped onto her bed.

"Are you marrying Maxwell because of our parents?"

"Yes," she said, rolling over and trying to go to sleep. She'd taken a pain pill when they got back to the apartment. Her head was pounding and she was certain it was from the champagne she'd consumed.

"Please, Julie, go away and let me sleep," she said.

"One more question and then I'll leave," she said. "Did Daddy tell you the business was in trouble and he needed Maxwell's money?"

Stunned that her sister knew, she raised up in bed and stared at her. "Yes, he told me that I had to marry Maxwell or else you, Sterling, and Mother would not be able to live the life you have now. I've got to marry Maxwell to save the family business."

Her sister nodded, a frown on her face. "All right, I'm leaving. Try to get some rest. I'm going to do some investigating. I think they're lying to you just so that you will marry who they want you to. But let me see what I can find out."

With that, her sister stepped out of the room. Julie was as smart as they came, and if anyone could find out the truth, she could. Could her father be lying to her just so he could keep control of her?

He knew she wasn't in love with Maxwell. Why would he do this to his daughter if he didn't need the money?

CHAPTER 20

*J*acob had been a monster for the last month. He'd been cranky and unbearable, and even his brothers were losing their patience with him, but he didn't care. All he wanted was to sit in his living room and stare at the painting up on the mantel.

Why the hell had this happened to him? Why had he been robbed and beaten and left for dead, only to meet the love of his life?

Only problem, she was promised to someone else.

As he sat on the couch, he sipped from his scotch. Had his mother gotten drunk to soothe some hidden pain? If so, he could understand why.

Oh, how he missed Hannah. The way she smelled, her laugh, the serious look on her face when she painted. So far he had not had the heart to get rid of her paintings or her trailer, though he had donated her old SUV.

If she came back, he'd buy her a new one.

All he could do was stare at the painting and wish Hannah were here beside him.

The smell of lavender filled his home and he groaned. The ghost refused to let him rest and came almost every night.

"Go away and leave me alone," he yelled. "I don't want any company, but most especially not you."

Oh, he was so miserable without Hannah that he just wanted to growl like a bear and scream at anyone who crossed his path.

"Watch your tone, young man, or I will show you some of my ghostly tricks," she said, appearing in front of him.

"Do your damage and get the hell out," he said, thinking she couldn't hurt him any worse than he was currently feeling.

She picked up his bottle of scotch and he groaned.

"Young man, I will toss this down that drain over there if you don't get up," she said. "It's time you stopped sitting there feeling sorry for yourself."

It had been a month since Hannah left with her father. A month of him sitting here every night drinking. He'd never imbibed so much alcohol in his life. His poor liver probably wished he'd get over her as well.

"And do what?"

"Go after her. You're being stubborn and mule-headed and just damn stupid for not going after what you want," she said.

"Sure, I'll just jump on a plane and go to New York City and stand in Times Square and yell *Hannah, I love you, where are you?* How many women do you think will answer my call."

"You're being ridiculous," she said. "I bet that cousin of yours, Tucker, could find her for you," she said.

Oh, most definitely, Tucker could find her, but she was engaged. In fact, she was probably getting married just any day, and that made him even angrier. Why should he be fighting for their love if she wasn't willing to stand up to her father and proclaim she wasn't going to marry Maxwell?

If she loved him, then why wasn't she fighting for them?

"What else have you got to say, Eugenia? So far, you haven't convinced me that I need to go running after her."

"Well, try this on for size. Do you love her? Miss her? Want her so bad, you can hardly stand it?"

Did she want him to bleed? Of course, he felt all those things and more. Every time he looked at her trailer, he wanted to cry. There were too many memories tied up with that old camper with the faded rainbow on the back. Too much unhappiness.

"Are you going to answer me?"

"Oh, yes, ma'am," he said sarcastically. "Can't you see I'm hurting?"

She chuckled. "That's why you need to do something. Give it one last try before it's too late. Any day now, she's going to marry that fella she doesn't love."

Every day, he thought about that wedding. Every day, he hated that today might be the day she walked down the aisle.

"I don't know her last name. I don't know how to find her," he said.

"Call your cousin, Tucker. Give it one more try. You might be surprised at how it ends."

"Oh, yeah, I could come back in even worse shape," he said.

Standing in front of him, she crossed her arms and he could see her ghostly eyes flashing with frustration.

"Or you could come home with Hannah on your arm," she said. "All of you Burnett boys are so damn stubborn. Now pick up that newfangled contraption you use to communicate and talk to your cousin."

Maybe Tucker could help him find her. He could take the jet and try one more time to reach her and convince her that he was the man for her. Maybe Eugenia was right. He should try to speak to her. What if she was hurting just as badly as he was?

"It's in the middle of the night in Germany," he said.

Kendra was on the last week of her tour and then they would be returning home.

"I don't care. You're running out of time. Contact him, now," she yelled. "Or regret this moment for the rest of your life. And I will make your life a living hell."

Damn, the ghost was getting upset. She'd already poured out two bottles of scotch over the last month. Now he hid his liquor from her.

"All right," he said and pulled out his new cell phone. "But if this goes badly, you will leave my house and not bother me any longer."

She smiled. "I'm not worried at all. You'll be seeing me again, soon."

What if Hannah didn't want him to interfere?

Dialing Tucker's number, a sleepy voice answered.

"About damn time you called me, though you could have chosen a better hour," he said. "It's three in the morning here."

Jacob glanced at his clock. It was eight in Texas.

"Sorry," he said. "Eugenia is driving me nuts and told me I had to call you."

Tucker chuckled. "Her name is Hannah Newhouse. Her father is Richard Newhouse III and he owns Newhouse Investments. The man she is going to marry tomorrow night is Maxwell Thomson. If you're going to stop this wedding, you better get your ass to New York."

He sighed. "What if she wants to marry this man?"

"You'll never know until you confront her. You've got less than twenty-four hours before this wedding takes place. For your own peace of mind, talk to her."

The sound of thunder rumbled from outside.

"Shit, it sounds like the weather is bad," he said.

"You're running out of time," Tucker said. "Go. Get to DFW. You may have to wait, but it's only a three-hour flight."

With a sigh, he knew he had to try.

"All right, thanks for your help. When did you investigate her?"

"When you were found," he said. "I didn't trust that a woman would pick up a man in the middle of the night alongside the road without knowing something about him. But Hannah took a chance on you, and for that, we'll be forever grateful."

Determination filled him. "She did. Now I have to get to her and see if she's willing to take a chance on us again."

"Good luck," Tucker said. "Now if you'll excuse me, I'm going to snuggle up against my wife and try to go back to sleep."

"Goodnight," Jacob said.

He disconnected the call and stared at the ghost who had been listening the entire time.

"I've got to see if I can catch a plane to New York. Her name is Hannah Newhouse. Are you satisfied?"

The ghost grinned at him. "I will be when you return with her and we plan your wedding."

Oh, great. What if she didn't want to come back with Jacob? What if she was happy to be marrying this Maxwell character?

"Let's just start with me getting to New York," he said.

A crackle of lightning lit the front yard and the lights went out.

"Great, it's going to storm," he said. "I'm calling the company pilot now to see when we can leave."

A few minutes later, he felt despair.

"I'm sorry, Mr. Burnett, but this storm system has DFW socked in. The earliest we can get out is in the morning. Let's meet up at DFW at eight o'clock."

The wedding was at three that afternoon. He had to be there before then.

"All right," he said. "See you then."

The smell of lavender still permeated the air as he went into the bedroom to pack a suitcase.

"I can't get out until eight in the morning," he said out loud. "The wedding is at three."

With the time difference, it would be cutting it close. Especially, if they had any more delays. Why had he waited so long to reach out to her?

What if he got there too late?

CHAPTER 21

*I*t was her wedding day. All morning, she'd been subjected to hairstylists and makeup artists in preparation for the ceremony at three o'clock this afternoon.

Night before last, Julie had come to her room and said she was going to do some investigating, but so far she'd not said another word.

With a sigh, Hannah tried to accept that she was going to be bound to Maxwell, though she didn't love him.

Last night, he'd been the perfect fiancé trying to be attentive at the rehearsal dinner. She'd sulked. Her father had threatened her if she misbehaved in front of Maxwell's family and friends.

Couldn't Maxwell see she didn't want to marry him? Couldn't he see that she wasn't in love with him? Or did he not care?

Was the damn job promotion more important than his own happiness?

At one o'clock, her mother came into her room. Her makeup was perfect, her hair looked divine. The newspaper would have stunning pictures of the wedding party if her mother had anything to say about it.

"It's time to leave for the church," she said. "This will all be over in a couple of hours and then you and Maxwell can jet off to your honeymoon."

Oh, yes, they were going to some tropical island and she couldn't care less. But more than anything, she was dreading the wedding night. The thought of sleeping with Maxwell left her cold.

Hannah smiled.

"Mother, did you love Dad when you married him?"

"Of course, dear," she said.

"Then why are you two making me marry a man, I don't love?" she said softly, hoping she could convince her to help her call off the wedding. "Why?"

"Now, Hannah, your father has told you the reason why. You want your sisters to have the same life you've been given. You want us all to live the lifestyle we're accustomed to?"

There it was, the guilt. *Give up your happiness, so we can continue to live this way and not suffer the embarrassment of all of New York society knowing we're broke.*

"You'll soon fall in love with Maxwell and then the babies will come. Just try to enjoy your married life, dear. Everything will be all right, you'll see," she said.

Hannah sighed and picked up the suitcase she had packed for her honeymoon while their maids carried down her dress and all the wedding paraphernalia.

The image of Jacob came to mind and she closed her eyes tightly. She couldn't think about him or her makeup would be ruined by her tears.

But how she wished it was him she was marrying. She would be so excited. So thrilled.

While sitting in the limo, it moved slowly toward the church in uptown, traffic crawling, taking her to her destiny. Her parents weren't particularly religious people, but they insisted she be married in a church.

Sighing, she said a little prayer.

Her sister sat across from her and she reached out and squeezed her hand. They had not been alone all morning and she wished that she could give her some hope, something.

When they arrived at the church, she got out of the limo and they went into the bride's room. There, her sisters and she dressed in their wedding finery and she tried not to cry.

This wedding was happening and there was nothing she could do to stop it. No matter how much she loved Jacob, she had to do this for her family.

She'd been threatened and told she would lose everything if she acted up.

Julie kept glancing at her, but their mother stayed right there in the room, making certain Hannah was not going to disappear.

A knock sounded at the door. "Is there a Julie Newhouse in here?"

"Yes," her sister said.

"Package for you," the lady said and handed her an envelope.

Julie took the package and disappeared. Hannah stared as her sister rushed out the door. Where was she going?

A few minutes, she came back, a grim expression on her face. She mouthed to Hannah, *We need to talk.*

Had she learned something?

Finally, at five minutes till three, her mother kissed her on the cheek. "Oh, Hannah, dear, you're a beautiful bride. Soon this will be over and you'll see that we made the right decision for you."

What could she say?

"Thanks, Mother," she said, knowing she would never agree that this was what she should do.

With a sad smile, her mother walked out the door and she heard music playing inside the church. It was almost time. Her father would meet her in the vestibule and walk her down the aisle.

"It's a lie," her sister said. "It's all a lie. They do not need the money according to the documents I just received. Father just wants you to marry Maxwell, so he can get part of their money too. If this is not what you want, don't do it."

Stunned, Hannah stared at Julie. "He would trade me just to make more money?"

Julie nodded slowly. "I'm sorry. I'm sure he will do the same thing to me and Sterling."

Fierce anger filled Hannah. She'd lost the love of her life because of him. She'd given up her paintings, everything she loved, so she could save the family business by marrying Maxwell and it was all a lie.

The only time she'd ever defied her father had been her forbidden trip. The one where she met Jacob. But right now, she was filled with rebellion.

There was a knock on the door and she hugged Julie and Sterling. It was time to go.

"What are you going to do?"

"I don't know," she said. "Hang onto your bouquets because trouble may be right around the corner."

Her sister grinned. "Love you, Hannah. Do what is best for you. Not what is best for Father."

Marrying Maxwell was not what was best for her.

In the corridor of the church, her father stood waiting. He took her by the arm.

"You're going to be very happy, Hannah. I know you don't believe it now, but Maxwell is perfect for you."

Her sisters and their groomsmen walked down the aisle. They were next.

"Tell me again, Daddy, why do you want me to marry Maxwell."

He glanced at her a strange look on his face.

"You're saving the family business," he said. "With Maxwell's money combined into the business, we'll be unstoppable."

Unstoppable? He didn't say that his sisters and mother would continue to live the lifestyle they were accustomed to. It was all so that he could make *more* money?

The doors opened and the wedding march began. People in the packed church stood as he led her down the aisle toward Maxwell, who stood grinning like an idiot at the front of the church.

The thought of sleeping with him sent a shudder down her spine.

"Who gives this woman away?"

"Her mother and I," her father said as he handed her off to Maxwell.

They walked up the stairs toward the altar and stood facing one another.

She leaned in to Maxwell. "I can't marry you."

A shocked look came over his face. "What?"

Unable to stop herself, she smiled at his reaction. "I don't love you. I can't marry you, and this wedding is being called off."

The preacher cleared his throat. "Is there a problem?"

She smiled at him, feeling lighthearted and happy for the first time in over a month. "Yes, I'm not marrying this man."

Her sister giggled.

Knowing in her gut that this was right, she turned and faced the crowd, feeling so relieved. "The wedding is off. So sorry." Not.

The sound of people chattering filled the church.

Her father roared with anger and her mother started to cry.

Just then the doors of the church crashed open and Jacob came running down the aisle. "Stop. You can't marry him. I love you."

A grin spread across her face and she lifted her skirts and ran to the man she loved. "Thank God, you're here. I just called the wedding off. I love you, Jacob. You're the only man I want to marry."

Her father stepped into the aisle. "I will cut you off. You won't receive another dime from me, do you understand?"

Jacob glanced at him. "Sir, respectfully, she doesn't need your money. I'm a *billionaire* with my own money. We'll be just fine. Now if you'll excuse me, we're leaving."

Shocked, her father's mouth dropped open and he gasped.

Glancing at Jacob, her heart swelled with love and she placed her hand in his. "Let's go. Take me anywhere but here."

A grin spread across his face, and together, they ran out of the sanctuary as the crowd stared in astonishment.

Grabbing her suitcase out of the bride's room, they hurried outside to the waiting limo.

Once they were inside, she saw her father, mother, and two sisters rush out of the church. She waved good-bye to them and then she turned to Jacob.

"I'm sorry I didn't tell you before my father arrived, but I didn't love Maxwell. My father insisted I marry him to save my family from being homeless. Right before the wedding, my sister told me it was all a lie to get me to marry who he wanted. Since I wasn't rescuing my family, I knew the wedding was off."

Jacob pulled her into his arms. "So you were going to marry him to help your family."

"Yes, he told me if I didn't my mother and sisters would suffer. He would lose his hedge fund and they would all be destitute."

Jacob shook his head.

"I ran away so I could take one last trip and fulfill my dreams before I was forced into a marriage I didn't want."

Leaning down, he kissed her on the mouth and it was the sweetest kiss she'd ever received.

When they broke apart, he stared into her eyes. "Hannah, I love you. I will never cheat on you, and I expect the same from you. If ever we have a problem, let's talk about it."

Love filled her heart. "Agreed. But you don't have to worry about me cheating on you. I love you with all my heart, and no one, not even my family will come between us."

He layered his mouth over hers, and this time, the kiss was full and complete and left her sighing.

"Where are we going? I want to get rid of this awful dress," she said. "I've hated it from the day my mother chose it."

A grin spread across his face.

"The family has a house on the beach. Would you like to spend a week there, just the two of us?"

"Oh, yes," she said. "Just you and me and sand."

"Yes," he said. "Though I did put an empty canvas and your paints on the company plane."

Her eyes lit up and tears filled her eyes. "I haven't painted since I left you in Texas."

"I'll even let you paint me nude," he said. "But be prepared to stop when I come after you."

A giggle erupted from her and warmth filled her. This felt right. This was what her life was supposed to be – her and Jacob together, loving one another.

"By the way," she said. "How do you feel about children?"

"Eventually, I want a family. Three or four kids," he said. "But right now, I just want you."

Laying her down in the seat, she sighed. "And I want you more than you'll ever know."

His lips descended on hers.

Finally, Hannah had grown a spine and told her father and Maxwell no. And, now, this man would love her and protect her until her dying day.

A stop on a lonely highway had brought her the love of her life.

CHAPTER 22

A month later, Jacob danced with Hannah at their wedding. The day had been filled with love and joy and more happiness than he'd thought possible. While he hated the fact that he'd almost died that night so long ago, he was grateful this woman saved him.

Her family had declined the invitation to their wedding, though her father had contacted him about putting some investments in his company. No, if the man couldn't come to his daughter's wedding, he wasn't going to invest with him.

Just no.

When they first met, she'd warned him about her father and now he knew what she meant. Her sister had sent her a video telling her how happy she was for her and how she wanted to attend, but her father refused.

Also she sent a gorgeous bouquet of flowers and a crystal vase for them. Even her younger sister had sent a gift. But not her mother and father. Oh well.

After they left New York that fateful day, they'd gone to

the beach, and there they had consummated their love. It had been a wonderful week that confirmed their feelings for one another.

It had given them time to seal their bond and prove they loved one another.

Now Jacob had two surprises waiting for his wife.

When the music stopped, he clinked a fork against a crystal glass. "Thank you, everyone, for being here today and supporting us and starting our life together with us. We love you. But I have a surprise for my lovely wife. Everyone, outside."

"Wait," Desiree said. "If you're leaving we need to shower you with birdseed."

A grin spread across his face. His cousin was always one for tradition.

Everyone gathered outside the door and they ran outside, being pelted by birdseed. It seemed like a silly tradition, but he would go along with it for Hannah's sake.

Racing outside, she stopped and gasped.

"Oh my goodness," she said.

He grinned at her. "That's right, darling. We're going to spend our honeymoon going to Abiquiu and Santa Fe and letting you complete your dream. Your paints are inside. We're packed up and ready to roll."

She stared at the massive RV he'd purchased. It was much nicer than the little travel trailer she'd bought. It was like a home on wheels.

"Jacob," she said, "you're going to help me fulfill my dream."

"Yes, darling, I am," he said.

"But what about yours?"

He grinned at her. "One more rodeo. One more and I'll be in the PBR world championship in Las Vegas in November. And once I've ridden there, I'm done."

She threw her arms around him. "I'm so scared for you, but I'll be right there supporting you."

Over the last month, the doctor released him, and she'd gone with him to two rodeos. Both times, he'd lasted past the buzzer. Both times, he'd avoided hitting his head. Both times, he walked away a winner.

"Once I get that gold buckle, I'm through," he said. "Then we'll travel wherever you want to go and paint."

She grinned at him. "I love you, Jacob Burnett. Thank God, I picked you up on that lonesome stretch of road."

"I thank him every day," he said. "Now come on, let's roll."

He helped her up into the RV, which his brothers and cousins had decorated with *Just Married* with bright window markers and tin cans hanging off the bumper. Condoms hung from the grill in the front and he knew those would soon be gone.

"Have a safe trip," Joshua called.

Aunt Rose stood outside waving, and the image of Eugenia stood beside her. She blew them a kiss and then she pointed to Justin.

Jacob couldn't help but laugh. His brother had no idea what was about to hit him. No idea at all. But if she did for his brother what she'd done for him, Justin would be a very lucky man.Though he knew his brother didn't believe in happily ever afters or ghosts.

* * *

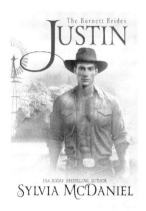

Can Justin Avoid Eugenia's Matchmaking and Remain a Bachelor?
Available at all Retailers!

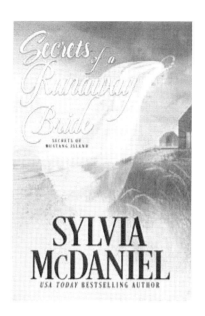

*A*t thirty-eight years of age, her time was running out to achieve the dream she so desperately wanted. Crystal Young yearned for a family she no longer had.

And yet sitting alone in the bridal waiting room, her anxiety was through the roof.

Was she making t

he right decision?

Yes, Aaron had agreed she could get pregnant immediately, so there was that point in his favor, but did she really love him? Love him enough to spend the rest of her life with him? Wake up beside him each morning?

Why did everything feel so off? Even her friends had told her this was not a good idea. Marriage was hard, and yet she wanted a normal family.

One that spent holidays together. One to go through life's misadventures, its fun moments, and even its worst times.

One where your father would walk you down the aisle, and your mother would help the first month after the grandchild was born.

A family to replace everything she'd lost and more.

With a sigh, she glanced at the clock. Their cruise ship would be leaving in two hours. Time to make a decision.

A decision that seemed to bear down on her like the weight of the planet. A decision that had serious consequences. To her, marriage was forever.

If this marriage was meant to be, shouldn't she be happy? Wouldn't she have gotten past the doubts? The anxiety?

Why did this feel so wrong?

A knock at the door had her jumping.

Standing, she scuttled to the door in the short silk dress she'd chosen. The dress was more for an after-five occasion, and yet she hadn't wanted the long-flowing gown. Nothing about this wedding was the same as she'd dreamed of years ago.

Opening the door, Spencer Duncan, Aaron's best friend stood in front of her. His eyes were dark and ominous and a serious expression graced his handsome face.

Aaron was backing out…

"May I come in?" Spencer asked.

"Of course," she said. "Is something wrong? Has Aaron changed his mind?"

Why did relief surge through her at the thought? Another signal that this wedding was all wrong.

"No," Spencer said, "but there's something you need to know before you agree to marry him. I've not slept the last two nights trying to decide whether to do what was right or keep my mouth shut. I've got to tell you the truth."

This sounded strange. What did she need to know?

Nervous, she licked her lips as an unwelcome tingle centered in the pit of her stomach. What kind of secrets was her fiancé hiding?

"Aaron has not been honest with you. He's in financial trouble, so his mother has basically bought him. She wants grandchildren, an heir. By marrying you, he can give her that and she'll pay off his debts."

That seemed odd. When they talked, he acted like he had plenty of money. And they couldn't wait to have children together. She wanted at least three and had to get started now before the clock ran out. It was one of the reasons she'd said yes to his proposal. And now she was doubting herself.

"I didn't know about his financial troubles, but we both want children," she said, alarm bells ringing as she suddenly thought about how Spencer was always around Aaron.

"Being with me, we could never have children unless we adopted," Spencer said. "His mother wants the family line to continue. She thinks you can *cure* him."

Like a smack to the forehead, she suddenly realized what was going on. How could she have been so blind?

"Aaron is your lover," she said breathlessly.

Spencer's shoulders relaxed and his posture completely changed. His expression softened and he seemed to turn into a different person, like the man she'd been introduced to not too long ago wasn't the real Spencer.

"Yes, darling, he is," he said, using a word he'd never used around her. "And he has no intention of giving me up," he said. "That's not fair to you or to me."

Stunned, she sank like a rock into the nearest chair. Her

dress slid up her thighs, but she didn't even try to pull it down. Nobody in this room was interested.

"All this time, I've wondered why he seemed aloof when it came to sex between us, and now I know why. He didn't want me; he wanted you," she said, hurt causing her chest to ache.

Aaron wanted another man, not her.

Spencer stood there, shaking his head. "Darling, I'm sorry to be the one to tell you, but this wedding is a huge mistake. And once you have the baby, the grandmother plans on fighting for custody. You will come out of this with nothing."

Now she understood all the feelings of doubt. The feelings of anxiety. The universe had been trying to warn her that she was making a colossal blunder, but she kept pushing forward. Pushing to get what she wanted, whether it was the right thing or not. Damn her determination.

When her chin fell to her chest, the first tear trickled down her cheek.

It wasn't like she was madly in love with Aaron. He was just a means to get what she wanted.

"I wish you had told me sooner," she said.

He hung his head for a moment. "I've been fighting with myself for the last month, and this week, it became unbearable. This morning, I knew I had to tell you."

Looking up at him, she saw tears in the corners of his eyes.

"Thank you for letting me know."

"If he learns I spoke to you, I'll lose him," Spencer said. "And his witch of a mother, she will cut him off for not getting what she wants."

There would be no wedding. There would be no baby in nine months. There would be no family. Her friends were gathered, waiting in the parlor for her to walk down the aisle, and now she couldn't face anyone.

Aaron was gay.

She'd almost married a gay man. It wasn't that she faulted him for being gay, just for lying to her and hiding the fact his mother would take any child they produced.

Crystal fought the overwhelming urge to curl up in a ball and cry her heart out, but there was no time.

The cruise. The honeymoon suite awaited them.

She needed time to think, to mend, and it was too late to cancel the trip she'd promised herself she would get pregnant on. She was getting on that boat. The limo sat out front of the mansion they were being married in.

Looking up, she gazed at Spencer. How had she missed all the telltale signs that he was gay? Aaron was gay. If he'd told her the truth, she would have wished him the best and walked away.

Now she felt humiliated that she'd refused to see the evidence when it was right in front of her face. She was a fool for letting herself believe she'd found a man who would love her and give her the family she longed for.

"Where's the back door?"

"Follow me," he said. "That's the way I came in."

She grabbed the carry-on bag she'd packed for tonight that held her white sexy nightie. Damn him.

Tears bubbled up, but she couldn't let go. Not yet. There would be plenty of time for crying once she got away. Right now, she had to escape. She had to part ways with this disastrous wedding. No wonder Aaron's mother had always looked at her like thinking *you poor fool*. Now she knew. Now she understood.

Looking around the room, she made sure she had everything. One more screw-up on her part. One more wrong choice.

It was time for her to forget her dreams. Time for her to face reality. She was meant to be alone.

"Let's go," she said.

When he opened the door, she heard the music. They were all waiting for her to walk down the grand stairs and say her vows. Well, they would be waiting until hell froze over.

Spencer peeked out of the bride's chamber, and together, the two of them tiptoed down the hall to the servants' stairs in the historic home in Galveston, Texas – a place she'd found on the internet not far from the cruise's docking station.

A ship she would be taking alone.

They hurried down the stairs. The caterers were busy setting up the food for the reception. She glanced at them. "Donate all of it to a homeless shelter."

"What?" the director said, her eyes growing large.

"Give the food to a homeless shelter. There will be no wedding today. There will be no reception. I'm leaving."

With that, she walked out of the kitchen and through the back door. After hurrying around to the front, she turned to Spencer when they reached the limo.

"Thank you for telling me. Tell Aaron I said…" What did she want to say to him? Only one thing came to mind and she didn't want to use that word. "Tell him I said don't ever contact me again. I wish him the best of luck. And Spencer you deserve better."

The man grinned. "If only I didn't love him."

"If he loved you, he would not have agreed to marry me," she said. "I hope you find someone who deserves you."

"You too," he said and hugged her.

She slipped the ring off her finger and handed it to Spencer. "Give it back to him, wear it, do whatever you want with that rock."

Gazing down at the jewelry in his hand, he shook his head, laughing. "It should have been mine."

"Yes, it should've been."

She climbed into the limo, closed the door, and rolled down the window to wave good-bye.

The door of the house opened and Aaron ran down the stairs, waving his arms wildly. "Stop. Where are you going? Spencer, you didn't tell her, did you?"

Shaking her head, tears filled her eyes. "Go, driver, now."

"Yes, ma'am," he said.

She pulled her mother's long white-lace wedding veil from her head as she sank against the leather seats. The car sped down the drive and pulled onto the street.

"Take me to the cruise ship," she told the driver. "At least one of us is going on our honeymoon."

Paperback Edition Available Everywhere!!
Or at www.SylviaMcDaniel.com

PLEASE LEAVE A REVIEW

Did you enjoy the book? Reviews help authors. I would appreciate you posting a review.

Follow Sylvia McDaniel on Facebook.

Sign up for my New Book Alert on my website and receive a complimentary book.

Contemporary Romance
Burnett Brides Contemporary Times
Travis
Tanner
Tucker
Joshua
Jacob
Justin

Return to Cupid, Texas
Cupid Stupid
Cupid Scores
Cupid's Dance
Cupid Help Me!
Cupid Cures
**Cupid's Heart
Cupid Santa
**Cupid Second Chance
Cupid Charmer
Cupid Crazy
Cupid's Bachelorette
Return to Cupid Box Set Books 1-3
Cupid Help Me Box Set Books 4-6
**The Unlucky Bride

Contemporary Romance
My Sister's Boyfriend
The Wanted Bride
The Reluctant Santa
The Relationship Coach

Secrets, Lies, & Online Dating

Bride, Texas Multi-Author Series
**The Unlucky Bride

Lipstick and Lead 2.0
Nailing the Hit Man
Nailing the Billionaire
Nailing the Single Dad

Secrets of Mustang Island
Secrets of a Summer Place
Secrets of a Runaway Bride
Secrets From the Past

The Langley Legacy
Collin's Challenge

Short Sexy Reads
Racy Reunions Series
Paying For the Past
Her Christmas Lie
Cupid's Revenge

Western Historicals
A Hero's Heart
Second Chance Cowboy
Ethan

American Brides
**Katie: Bride of Virginia

Angel Creek Christmas Brides
Charity
Ginger
Minnie
Cora

The Burnett Brides Series
The Rancher Takes A Bride
The Outlaw Takes A Bride
The Marshal Takes A Bride
The Christmas Bride
Boxed Set

Lipstick and Lead Series
Desperate
Deadly
Dangerous
Daring
**Determined
Deceived
Defiant
Devious
Lipstick and Lead Box Set Books 1-4
**Quinlan's Quest

Mail Order Bride Tales
**A Brother's Betrayal
**Pearl
**Ace's Bride

Scandalous Suffragettes of the West

**Abigail
Bella
Mistletoe Scandal

Southern Historical Romance
A Scarlet Bride
Charity

The Cuvier Women
Wronged
Betrayed
Beguiled
Boxed Set

** **Denotes a sweet book.**

**Want to learn about my new releases before anyone else?
Sign up for my New Book Alert and receive a free book.**

USA Today Best-selling author, Sylvia McDaniel obviously has too much time on her hands. With over eighty western historical and contemporary romance novels, she spends most days torturing her characters. Bad boys deserve punishment and even good girls get into trouble. Always looking for the next plot twist, she's known for her sweet, funny, family-oriented romances.

Married to her best friend for over twenty-five years, they recently moved to the state of Colorado where they like to hike, and enjoy the beauty of the forest behind their home with their spoiled dachshunds Zeus and Bailey. (Zeus has his own column in her newsletter.)

Their grown son, still lives in Texas. An avid football watcher, she loves the Broncos and the Cowboys, especially when they're winning.

www.SylviaMcDaniel.com
Sylvia@SylviaMcDaniel.com
The End!

Made in United States
North Haven, CT
18 April 2025

68069739R00113